SABOTAGED
NIGHTINGALE, VOLUME 1

EG MANETTI

A THIRTEEN SYSTEMS NOVELLA

Copyright

©2025 by Buniac Entertainment, LLC.
With the exception of quotes used in reviews, this book may not be reproduced, transmitted, or used in whole or in part by any means without the written permission of Buniac Entertainment.
All rights reserved.
This is a work of fiction. Names, characters, places, and incidents are the products of the author's imagination and used fictitiously. Any resemblance to actual persons, living or dead, events, or locales is entirely coincidental.
ISBN: 978-1-7375301-9-0

More of EG's Books

Read the award-winning science fiction series that launched the *Nightingale*.

The Twelve Systems Chronicles

The Cartel: The Apprentice, Volume 1
Bright Star: The Apprentice, Volume 2
Art of Stealth: The Apprentice, Volume 2.5
Transgressions: The Apprentice, Volume 3
Fortuna: The Apprentice, Volume 4
Serengeti Valor: The Apprentice, Volume 5
Nightingale: The Apprentice, Volume 6
Bond Proof: The Apprentice, Volume 7
Chalice Bearer: Thornraven, Volume 1
Shield Bearer: Thornraven, Volume 2
Thorn Bearer: Thornraven, Volume 3

The adventures continue in the Thirteen Systems.

Thornscore

CHRYS: Thornscore, Volume 1
FLETCHER: Thornscore, Volume 2
MALCON: Thornscore, Volume 3

Award-winning urban fantasy in near-future New England.

The Hidden Realms

Elemental Fire: The Hidden Realms, Volume 1

In Memory

John Thomas Berley
Who was and will always be my friend.

Contents

List of Characters i
The Thirteen Systems iii
1. Ill Luck 1
2. Strange Lands 12
3. Hidden Depths 27
4. Scientists and Sabotage 53
5. Genetic Memory 67
6. Toxin and Terrier 87
7. Star Bred Terrier 101
8. The Ancients 112
About EG 125

List of Characters
BRIGHT STAR

The Serengeti Group

Blooded Dagger Cartouche—Vistrite

Lucius Mercio, monsignor—preeminence of Serengeti and Blooded Dagger

Lilian Thornraven—protégé and consort (former apprentice)
Bran Hyssop—Raleigh's business partner and first officer of the *Nightingale*
Clarence—lieutenant, *Nightingale*, zoologist
Nickolas Cyncad—first lieutenant, *Nightingale*
Raleigh, Eleventh System deacon—mercium agent to the Eleventh and Twelfth Systems, captain of the *Nightingale*
Trevelyan, seigneur—Serengeti and Blooded Dagger security-privilege

Grey Spear Cartouche—Logistics and Distribution

Hercules Mehta, monsignor—preeminence of Grey Spear

Iron Hammer Cartouche—Controller Fabrication

Elenora Odestil, monsignor—preeminence of Iron Hammer

The Matahorn Alliance

Broken Blade Cartouche

Horatio Margovian, monsignor—preeminence of Broken Blade and Matahorn

William, seigneur —Bright Star (Horatio's son and heir)
Adriana Pepys, lieutenant commander, *Nightingale*—lead zoologist, *Nightingale*
Govind—ensign, *Nightingale*, zoologist
Imogen—chief medic, *Nightingale*
Lochan—security chief, *Nightingale*

The Leonardo Society

Steel Spike Cartouche

Angus Blackthorn, monsignor—preeminence of Steel Spike and Leonardo

   Tricia—ensign, *Nightingale,* entomologist

Other

Evander—Adriana's ex and member of the warrior class

THE FIVE WARRIORS & ADELAIDE of Antiquity

Socraide Omsted—*the First Warrior*. His dominion was three of the four habitable planets in the First System. His obsession with Adelaide Warleader turned the Three Systems from anarchy to order.

Rimon Ben Claude—*the Second Warrior*. His dominion was the two habitable planets of the Second System.

Mulan Tsao—*the Third Warrior*. Her dominion was Artesia in the First System.

Jonathan Metricelli—*the Fourth Warrior*. His dominion was the vistrite worlds, Metricelli Prime and Deuce in the Third System. After the Order of the Five Warriors was established, Jonathan's heirs added Desperation in the Sixth System to the Blooded Dagger holdings. It is the only other vistrite world in the Twelve Systems.

Sinead Standingbear—*the Fifth Warrior*. Her dominion was the one non-vistrite world in the Third System, Sinead's World.

***Adelaide Warleader—an ancient hero*.** During the Anarchy, she was Jonathan Metricelli's chief retainer and possible consort. During the early years of the Order of the Five Warriors, she was Socraide Omsted's consort and possible spouse.

The Thirteen Systems

First System

Socraide Prime
- Matahorn Alliance Headquarters
- Adriana Pepys world of origin and family home.

Socraide Deuce
Atlantis
Artesia

Second System

Rimon Prime
Rimon Deuce

Third System

Metricelli Prime
- Serengeti Headquarters
- Vistrite Crevasse

Metricelli Deuce
- Vistrite Crevasse

Sinead's World

Fourth System

Fortuna
- Leonardo Society Headquarters
- Construction site for the *Nightingale*

Fifth System

Troy

Sixth System

Desperation
- Vistrite Crevasse

Seventh System

    Edda

Eighth System

    Camelot

Ninth System

    Genji

Tenth System

    Hebrides
- Moons of uninhabitable Gemini
- Black and gray commerce financial center

Eleventh System

    Redemption
- Bran Hyssop's world of origin and family home
- Matahorn supply depots

Twelfth System

    Solace
- Matahorn supply depots

Thirteenth System

    Bright Star Prime
    Bright Star Deuce

1. Ill Luck

Sevenday 31, Day 5

Fingers racing over the pilot's console, Bran willed the yellow warning lights to disappear. In the viewer, fluffy, blue-tinged clouds whirled around the falling DOP-C. "Come one sweet one. Pull out. You can do it."

The whirling slowed. The yellow lights shifted to blue. Still too fast. Adjusting the trajectory, he managed to get the small transport to level out. "Well done, bella."

The choking sound from his passenger sounded suspiciously like laughter. Keeping his eyes split between the console and the viewer, he said, "There is nothing amusing about a propulsion malfunction."

Adriana's dry tones answered, "You named the cargo vessel?"

He glanced over his shoulder. "What say you?"

The slashes of her eyebrows rose over dark, liquid eyes. "Bella?"

Did I say that? Probably. "It is not a name. Means beauty."

Her lips twitched. "So, you do not name your transports but simply attempt to seduce them?"

A small chuckle escaped him. For a scientist, Adriana Pepys had a decent sense of humor. It was one of her many attractive attributes. "Chatting with the transport is a freighter pilot's habit. Comes from sevendays alone in the beaconed expanse."

"Well, it seemed to respond." She fingered the chair restraints. "I rescind my protest against the harness."

"It is not only your safety. The weight of your body flying around in the cargo area could hinder my ability to level out. As it is, we are going to land. I need to check the systems and it cannot wait until we reach our destination."

Adriana peered across the empty cargo area to the far window, where the clouds were parting to reveal purple plains edged with a dark green-and-red forest. "I thought these DOP-Cs were reliable."

"They *are* reliable." The Damaris Orbit to Planet Carrier, known as a DOP-C, was designed to enter and exit a planet without a launch platform. Lightweight, it could ascend, breach the atmosphere, and reach a low-orbit rendezvous point. It was perfect for shuttling passengers and cargo from the *Nightingale* to the planet's surface and back again. "I cannot remember a propulsion module ever malfunctioning outside of a test environment."

She huffed a small sigh. "The same is true of my instruments. And yet, the samples from last sevenday are so much goop."

Accidents and systems failures had beset the *Nightingale* and her crew since its return to the Thirteenth System after completing post-battle repairs in the Fourth System. The pilot scheduled to take Adriana to the surface had slipped on a wet spot in the mess hall and sprained her wrist. Otherwise, Bran would not be piloting the small cargo vehicle.

As first officer, he managed the logistics for all the exploration teams. But they needed the results of zoological studies, and he could justify the excursion. That he was eager for some time alone with the lovely but distant scientist was a bonus. "Unfortunately, your collection expedition may be delayed. If I cannot correct the problem, Captain Raleigh will need to send a flyer with repair equipment."

She frowned. "How far off are we?"

"At least a hundred miles west."

"That area has not been surveyed."

On this section of plains, only the high-altitude topographical mapping was complete. During the second stage, the low-altitude surveys included geological scans identifying minerals, precious metals, and subterranean water sources. Only after an area had completed the second stage were the scientists allowed to descend to sample water sources and geological deposits, and catalog flora and fauna. Landing in unknown terrain risked hidden hazards, but with over half the plains grid-mapped and sampled, they had found minimal variation. It was not ideal, but Bran had no other option. "It is still part of the plains. Landing will be safe enough."

From her expression, Adriana was far more concerned about her samples than her safety. "I have every confidence in you, Commander."

Her compliment fed his belief that she shared his attraction. At first, he had been wary of the Matahorn zoologist. Not from her actions but, because like all the inhabitants of the Eleventh and Twelfth Systems, he loathed her cartel for its callous and exploitive commerce tactics. Over the months, he had come to admire her, and the attraction intensified. Having passed his fiftieth year, he was no callow youth, and no one had stirred him so in over a decade. He was determined to attract her interest or confirm it was impossible.

He forced his attention back to the console, and away from the lovely fortysomething scientist. And she was lovely. Adriana's heavy-lidded eyes seemed huge in her triangular face. The contrast between her narrow chin and wide, sharp cheekbones was softened by a lush, full-lipped mouth. But it was the intelligence in her intense expression that elevated her features from pretty to compelling. Days of fieldwork had added bronze highlights to her tawny complexion and worn away some flesh, leaving the slate-gray uniform looser than at the voyage's start. He found her no less appealing for the loss of some voluptuousness.

The console lights shifted into pink and green, the landscape below taking on definition. Stroking the controls, he positioned the DOP-C for landing. Forty feet. Twenty. The console flared red. A sharp sound from the propulsion module was followed by a violent shudder. The purple ground roared up, the shock of impact slamming him back and then forward into the console and blackness.

***

Adriana's head throbbed. She wondered if she had overindulged at the Five Warriors' Festival. But no, that was not possible. The festival was months away. And she was on the *Nightingale*. In the Thirteenth System. Memory flooded past the pain, fear snapping open her eyes.

She was half hanging in her flight harness, the DOP-C on its side. Her hands reached for the harness fasteners and stopped. She was a scientist: observe and gather facts, analyze, hypothesize, and conclude.

The air in the vessel was clear. No smoke or chemical smells. Through the windows that were now the floor, she could see the springy purple vegetation that covered the plains in this section of the continent. Commonly known as Bright Star Deuce heather, the stuff was fibrous and dense enough to have cushioned their abrupt drop. The DOP-C's shell appeared to be intact. Nothing intruded from the planet.

She flexed her arms and legs, setting off a series of aches, but everything worked. Raising her hands to her head, she found no blood or lumps. The throbbing was probably due to the percussion of landing. Bracing against the arm of her chair, she released the harness and dropped free. The cabin was narrow enough that she had to duck to clear the seat. Somewhere, there was a mechanism to retract it against the wall in the same way as the other three seats. She would worry about that later.

Bran was unconscious, lolling on the downside of his fixed chair, one hand scraping wall, now floor. Only the harness kept him in place. Blood trickled from his forehead and along the side of his face. *Med kit.* Somewhere there was a med kit. Her aching head refused to give up the information. Gripping the chair, she forced herself to focus.

Her medic mother had taught Adriana first aid almost as soon as she learned to read. Working her way to the cargo section, she blessed the designer who built storage into the walls and thanked the Five Warriors that the DOP-C had rolled onto the side containing the med kit. She could reach the storage compartments above her head, but it would be difficult to release the contents without something to stand on.

Pulling the med kit free, she found the injector, and managed to jab herself. In moments the fuzziness cleared, and she could think. She could also move without her muscles protesting.

Stroking the side of Bran's face, she tried to rouse him. "Commander... Bran..."

When he did not respond, she activated the medic's scanner. Pushing aside his shaggy, silver-streaked sandy hair, she examined the cut on his forehead. Beneath it, a knot had formed, but the bone scan showed no fractures. Gently lifted eyelids revealed irises reacting to light. Cleansed of blood, the shallow cut was already closing. Rifling the med kit, she located bone sealant and the injector. The slick green paste could be applied over superficial wounds and would not exacerbate any brain swelling. An injection of pain inhibitors, healing stimulants, and nutrients took no more than a moment.

The scanner showed no hidden wounds or bone fractures, but enough subcutaneous hemorrhaging to promise a wealth of bruises. His neck and spine were intact. She needed to get him down. It was not more than a three-foot drop, but Bran was almost six feet, giving him four inches and at least a stone on her. She might slow his drop, but she could not lift him. Piling the two sets of camp bedding beneath his chair, she created six inches of cushion.

With cautious fingers she released his harness, bracing for his weight. His shoulders went first, over the edge of the chair. Grabbing his belt, she pulled against his momentum. It was graceless and would probably hurt her drug-numbed muscles, but she got him down with something approaching gentleness.

Crouched next to him, she scanned the tight buttocks and parts of his thighs the chair had blocked. More bruising but no other injuries. She slid a pillow under his head and turned it knot-side up. He had landed in the center of the bedding, his legs sprawled in a pattern that looked uncomfortable. After straightening them, she turned to examine the control console. Half the lights were out, including communications. There should be an emergency beacon in the compartment that held the med kit. She did not recall seeing it, but she had not been thinking about it.

Ten minutes of fruitless searching left her frustrated and battling fear. She needed to think for a moment. Opening a water vial, she settled on the area of bedding not holding Bran. Giving him the pain inhibitor may have been an error. It was probably keeping him unconscious.

There was no question, the *Nightingale*'s first officer was far too attractive for her peace of mind. Under his wide brow, angular masculine features included a strong jaw and deep-set amber eyes. Coupled with a lean, fit body, and sharp intellect, his presence generated a visceral reaction of appreciation and desire.

Rolling the cool water vial between her palms, she attempted to erase the silky feel of his hair, the warm satin of his back. Moisture beaded on the small dark contraception mark at the base of her thumb. With Bran the only member of the crew who piqued her interest, it had been foolish to bother with the injection. But some part of her insisted the two of them might find their way to intimacy.

When she joined the *Nightingale* a year ago, she was eager to flee the humiliation of her failed consort alliance. For the warrior elite, wedlock alliances were commerce treaties blending wealth and genetics. A consort alliance was a common alternative to wedlock that allowed for a partner of lower rank and without warrior genetics. Offspring of consort alliances were ranked among the warrior elite and included in the warrior family. Unlike wedlock alliances, consort alliances could be dissolved.

Everyone at Matahorn Headquarters knew Evander had set aside his commoner consort to take a warrior spouse. Joining the *Nightingale* to explore the first new system in over two centuries was an ideal means to escape gossip without the appearance of fleeing.

She knew to be wary of rival Serengeti's crew members, especially the free-trader Captain Raleigh. He was a last-minute replacement when brave Captain Jarrod was killed defending Bright Star. Distant kin to the Mercio family that governed Serengeti, Raleigh's exemplary record in the pirate actions made him acceptable to Adriana's cartel, the Matahorn Alliance.

She had been astounded to discover the Serengeti first officer was also a free-trader from the Eleventh System. She had been shocked by the way her senses reacted to his presence. Bran had served under Raleigh's command, and according to the Matahorn dossier, lost his wife in one of the first pirate raids. She pitied his loss, and under horrific circumstances. But that did not change that he was pilot and navigator on free-trader freighters. A smuggler. By the standards of the First System, not more than a step removed from a pirate. She assumed some Serengeti intrigue placed him in the command crew.

An assumption that was eroded by experience. Bran proved to be far different from the nefarious free-traders depicted in entertainments, with their constant use of contractions and other vulgar behavior. During the months of training and the voyage to the Thirteenth System, she came to admire his competence and fairness. She even discovered a dry sense of humor beneath his reticence.

The *Nightingale* had barely begun exploration of the two planets when the despoiler fleet attacked. During the harrowing day and a half of cat-and-mouse before the armada arrived, Bran had demonstrated a warrior's courage and fortitude. Of course, emotion could be swaying her. In the two years since the termination of her consort alliance, he was the only man to appeal to her.

She had been having variations of the same mental conversation for months without resolution. Before the crash, she had hoped a day with the man would resolve her conflicting emotions. Now, she was far more concerned about their survival.

***

Bran woke to a pounding head, and a mouth that tasted like mulch. He had experienced enough injuries to recognize the aftermath, but he had no recall of the event. Dragging open gummy eyes, he blinked against the light streaming from the DOP-C window above him.

Cyclops turds. The crash. "Adriana?"

His voice was a hoarse croak. The woman's silence was disquieting. Turning his head toward her seat, he found it empty, the harness dangling. His hand hit an object, rattling it against the floor. A water vial. Lurching to a sitting position, he ripped off the seal and downed half of it in three swallows. Whatever else, the zoologist was uninjured. There was no other explanation for his position on the floor or the conveniently placed water.

There was also his relative lack of pain. He remembered hitting the console. Brushing hair back from his forehead, his fingers skimmed against bone sealant. It was dry and smooth. Judging from that, and the position of the sun, it neared midday. He had been out for at least half a period.

Long enough for Adriana to act as medic. It was obvious that she had some training, although clearly, she did not have enough training in exploration protocols. She should not have left the DOP-C. He would deal with her foolishness as soon as he alerted the *Nightingale* to their situation.

The communications section of the pilot's console was dark. The emergency beacon would have to suffice. Finding his feet, he made his way to the storage compartments.

He expected a scientist to be neater. The food and water were in the area used by the bedding that was now in the cabin. The medic's kit was in the water section. The weapons locker was open and a fireburst pistol was missing. Not so foolish, then. But what had she done with the emergency beacon?

Adriana's voice came from above. "It is not there."

Turning, he saw her face peering through the open door. "What say you?"

"You seek the emergency beacon. It is not there. I searched all the compartments I could reach."

That explained the mess. "What are you doing out there?"

Her nose wrinkled and her lips curved in wry smile. "Biological imperative."

She motioned to an area over his head. "Even if I could get the freshener open, and pull myself into it, there is gravity to consider."

He snorted a laugh, somewhat amazed at her humor in the dire circumstances. Following her gesture, he noticed the other storage compartments. "You did not search these?"

"I am tall enough to open them, but not release the contents. And there was the risk the contents broke loose during the crash. I wished no damage to myself or our supplies."

He reached up. "It would take more than a twenty-foot fall and a roll to break the clamps."

Her face disappeared, and her feet appeared, dangling in the opening. She wriggled and her toes found the pilot's chair. Using her improvised step, she dropped into the cabin. Her movements drew his attention to a cargo restraint that was tied to her former seat and ran up through the opening.

"What is the purpose of the line?"

"Climbing rope. To scale the outside. I might manage the drop without injury, but getting back up is another matter."

The woman was resourceful. Far more than he would have expected of a pampered First System dweller.

Her dark eyes filled with concern. "I checked you for injuries. Nothing was broken. No internal injuries. Sprains or other ills?"

Bran slid the compartment door open. "I ache all over and my head hurts. You?"

"Aches are the worst of it." When nothing fell out of the exposed compartment, she joined him. Looking up, she shook her head. "Nothing but my equipment and sample kits."

He reached for the door of the other compartment but was not optimistic. "This section holds a repair kit and tools. I doubt the beacon could fit."

Adriana stepped behind him, clearly unconvinced nothing would tumble out.

"Five Warriors' Grace."

Adriana rose on her toes to peer into the compartment. "The beacon?"

"No, but the repair kit and tools are secure." He reached up to release the kit. "It will take a while, but I should be able to get communications functioning."

"How long a while?"

"A few bells." He lowered the kit. "I will not know for certain until I get the console open."

"Can you grab my instruments and sample case?"

"For what purpose?" He turned to look at her. "You cannot go out there alone."

"Of course I can." She cocked her head. "We landed in the plains. This section may not have been mapped, but I doubt it contains anything more hazardous than what we have already discovered. None of the local predators are dangerous until sunset. That is several bells away."

He shook his head. "We cannot know that."

She patted the holstered pistol. "I can disintegrate the head of a plains' rodent at ten paces. I will be fine."

"Do I need to remind you that I outrank you?"

"Need I remind you that we are three months behind on our mission? We are here and not leaving soon. I have a duty to fulfill."

Stubborn woman. As much as he disliked it, Adriana had a point. The *Nightingale* had barely begun exploration of the Thirteenth System's two planets when the despoiler fleet attacked. The armada of Serengeti's preeminence, Lucius Merico, arrived and defeated the despoilers, but it was a vicious battle. The *Nightingale*, along with the half of the armada that survived, limped back to the Fourth System and Fortuna for repairs. Repairs that should have been completed in two sevendays but had dragged on for six. Another two sevendays returning, and now the endless accidents and delays.

They were more than three months behind schedule. A schedule that promised investors the opportunity to bid on land tracts and mining licenses in the new year that was only four months away. Even more essential was the unspoken imperative to determine if Deuce held vistrite deposits.

The most precious substance in the Thirteen Systems, vistrite crystals were essential to all advanced technology. Only two of the Thirteen Systems held vistrite, the last deposit found more than eight hundred years ago. While the six separate vistrite crevasses ran for hundreds of miles and fell to depths of up to thirty miles, everyone knew the supply was not infinite. If society was to avoid another Anarchy, they needed to discover new sources. The entire crew was devastated when none was found on Bright Star Prime. With Deuce not yet half mapped, there was still hope. The faster they moved through the grids, the faster they would locate the substance if it was anywhere on the planet.

Hefting the repair kit, he set it by the console. "Let me inspect the terrain."

2. Strange Lands

Sevenday 31, Day 5-Continued

Before Adriana could begin her sampling, she spent a period standing guard while Bran examined the exterior of the DOP-C. She felt a bit foolish holding a pistol at the ready against the small mammals that inhabited purple vegetation, but he was being reasonable, and she did enjoy his company. Although scuffed and dented, the vehicle remained sealed.

Satisfied with the DOP-C's soundness, Bran climbed back up and lifted a distance-viewer to his eyes. Part of the DOP-C supplies, the device was smaller than the ones issued with the *Nightingale*. Curious, she asked, "How far can they reach?"

His head turned slowly as he examined their surroundings. "Ten thousand feet."

"How is that possible? They are so small."

His head stopped moving and he lowered the device. His eyes were hard. "Due to Matahorn greed, vistrite costs in the Eleventh and Twelfth systems are at least twice that of the First System. We have become innovative out of necessity."

Bridling at the attack on her cartel, Ardriana snapped, "Funding a new system was as exorbitant an undertaking two centuries ago as it is today. The free-traders did not have the funds and needed Matahorn. They agreed to repay that investment with the import-export fees."

"Fees that grew exponentially while the governing council turned a blind eye."

"That was Omar Petrovich and his despoilers. That is all changed, now."

Bran's harsh laughter held no humor. "That villain was in control for a handful of decades. Not centuries. And it has only changed because he was discovered and Matahorn forced into reparations."

"That is not true." She must have been deranged to find him attractive. "Monsignor Horatio was appalled to discover one of his warriors was so corrupt. He did not challenge the reparations."

Snorting, Bran raised the viewer to his eyes. "This is a pointless conversation."

She could not agree more. "The past is past. It is the here and now that holds our duty. The supply depots are under free-trader control, and we are all part of the *Nightingale*."

The last was a bit of a stretch. Her second in zoology, Lt. Clarence, was from Serengeti and gave her minimal acknowledgment. Certainly, he did not consider them as part of a unified crew. Lazy and inept, his familial connections in Blooded Dagger, Serengeti's ruling cartouche, won him a place on the *Nightingale*. His most recent debacle involved classifying a species of river snail as indigestible when it was, in fact, toxic. She had reached a point where she could not trust him with anything but the most minor tasks, which compelled her to make this ill-fated excursion for replacement samples.

Bran lowered the viewer and offered her an oblique glance. She thought he would speak, but instead he returned to scanning.

Glad of her sunshades, Adriana followed his path.

Behind them and to the west, massive midnight-blue mountains were capped with white that held the same hint of blue as the clouds. They were much larger than she had realized when she saw them from a hundred miles east. Even now, as close as they appeared, she knew they were miles away.

East and south, the purple plains flowed to the horizon in shallow waves that would solidify into rolling hills upon close inspection. From a distance, Deuce heather was a dark lavender mass. Close up, the diamond-shaped leaves were variegated, ranging from palest lilac to deep violet. The plants rustled with the breeze and the movements of the small animals that dwelled beneath them. There was no sign of the elk-like grazers that roamed the plains in herds. So far, Adriana's team had classified two-score mammal species and twice that in insects and birds, but she was certain there were more.

No more than a quarter mile to the north, the plants gave way to a forest of red and ocean-green trees that ran along the horizon. According to the lead botanist, the red trees were conifers and he had identified three different varieties. Like the Deuce heather, the green trees were deceptive. Deciduous, there were seven distinct varieties varying in hue from dark blue to fern-green. The lead botanist had been unable to catalog further, as beset by troubles as the rest of the expedition—the same troubles that had hindered the zoologists' attempts to explore beyond the plains. All they knew of the forest's inhabitants were avians spotted from the plains and larger predators they noted emerging with the dark.

In an attempt to accelerate their lagging schedule, Adriana had brought some live specimens aboard the *Nightingale*. All were lost to some strange plague within a sevenday. Inconclusive tests left her hypothesizing that something in the *Nightingale*'s environment was toxic to the animals. She was seeking the exact cause when an equipment malfunction liquefied the genetic samples that they had extracted before the plague.

Until Adriana understood the source of the plague, she could not transport more specimens onto the *Nightingale*. Instead, she would return to the slower trap-and-release protocol. Once she had extracted genetic samples, she would tag the creatures with subdermal trackers.

Lowering the viewer, Bran jerked a nod. "Stay within a few paces of the DOP-C. I will let you know when I have restored communications."

Shifting her position, Adriana prepared to drop back into the cargo vessel for her equipment.

Bran held up a hand. "Stay here. I will hand you your kit."

It was surprisingly gracious after their disagreement. Quite possibly the often taciturn first officer's attempt at an apology. Beaming a smile, she scrambled out of his way, admiring the way his biceps strained his tunic sleeves when he lowered himself into the cabin.

***

With the last of her supply cases lowered to the ground, Adriana took a final peek through the open door. Bran was wedged half under the console, displaying a very fine set of buttocks as he twisted to access his target. There was no question that he filled out his slate-gray uniform in a manner that sent her mind to carnal fantasies.

Free-trader. Serengeti. Her failed consort alliance should have broken her of longing for unattainable men. As it had for the past two years, bitterness rose with the memory. She had been so thrilled when Evander had offered a consort alliance. A warrior from a cadet branch of Matahorn's ruling family—the Margovians—he was charming, handsome, and artistic.

Her family was wealthy and well respected, but for a shy scientist from the second-level elite it had seemed a romance had come to life. A romance that ended on a sevenday's notice when Evander found another he preferred. A warrior and a signet heir, the woman was a far more advantageous alliance than Adriana. When Adriana protested, asked what had happened to his love, he laughed, saying, "Do not be a child. Love is entertainment. Marriage is commerce."

Clenching her jaw, she forced the memory away. *Duty.* She had animals to trap and release. The area below the rope was flattened and gouged from the DOP-C's rough landing. Beyond it, the springy plants reached her knees. They gave off an odd spicy-sweet scent reminiscent of a blend of ginger and tarragon. Many of the crew found it unpleasant, but Adriana liked it. Reveled in the otherness. The alienness.

How alien? That was the question. Every analysis indicated that the ancients who had terraformed more than half the Twelve Systems had been at work here.

Opening the first case, she removed a small lure. Every schoolchild knew that before the three centuries of warfare known as the *Anarchy*, a vast and enlightened empire had existed. When a millennia ago the Five Warriors had imposed order on the Anarchy, they were too late to preserve more than fragments of the ancients' knowledge and technology.

A tap to the control pad, and the lure sailed three paces, dropping into the purple without leaving a broken leaf or scent marker.

After five centuries of order, when the original three systems had become seven, scholars and technologists realized that so many habitable planets would not form randomly. Somehow, before disappearing, their ancient ancestors had seeded their legacy throughout the galaxy.

Moving clockwise, she set another three lures. Adriana was a scientist. She could not allow bias in her research, but even the most skeptical accepted that Bright Star Prime and Deuce would not be so habitable without some terraforming intervention.

Two more lures were in position. If her hypothesis proved correct, the creatures of the Thirteenth System were genetic cousins—if not siblings—of species common in the other twelve systems.

She set the last five lures, completing a half circle, and turned for the DOP-C. Although the lures did not leave scent markers, her movements would have scattered her scent in a wide area. It could be a period before her scent faded and the lures attracted the little creatures.

***

Bran forced shoulders tight with anger to relax. Even before the evidence of the loosened communications controllers, he knew the DOP-C had been sabotaged. He and Raleigh had designed the vehicles and tested them thoroughly. This was a third-generation transport, and the systems did not fail. For some time, they had suspected that many of the incidents slowing progress were not ill luck, but malfeasance.

Now, he was certain. They had a traitor on the *Nightingale*. Maybe more than one.

Before departing for the day's mission, Raleigh had instructed Bran to watch Adriana. She had the skills to orchestrate several of the incidents, and if the sabotage was a Matahorn intrigue, she could well be their saboteur.

Bran had protested. He had spent enough time with the woman to know that while she was clever enough, she was far too forthright and honorable to make an adequate stealth operator. Nor could he imagine the woman who grieved over dead specimens would have done aught to destroy them. Raleigh had remained skeptical, but there could be no doubt now. Both Adriana and Bran could have died in the crash.

The notion sent another wave of rage washing through him. He had lost his wife to pirates. He would not lose another woman. *Lose another woman?* Bran's fingers went still. When had she become so important? She could not be more different from his wife. Odette had been an artist, quick to laugh, quick to anger, and quick to forgive—her every thought and emotion on display.

Adriana was thoughtful and contained. She had a quick wit and dry sense of humor that appealed to him, but none of his wife's effervescence. And yet, she stirred him on a visceral level. Knowing they would be months, mayhap years, on the *Nightingale,* he had moved slowly, building their friendship before seeking passion. The last thing he wanted was for matters to become awkward.

But those months and years could be an illusion. Adriana could have died in the crash, and he would have lost the opportunity forever.

Adjusting his grasp on the diagnostic tool, Bran refocused on the damaged communications system. Before aught else, he needed to see them rescued.

***

Adriana climbed up onto the DOP-C. A glance inside showed Bran was still half under the pilot's console.

Closing her eyes against the sun's glare, she thought again how much she had missed fieldwork while allied with Evander. Even with the dangerous crash, this day was far more enjoyable than the endless days in the halls of Matahorn Headquarters dealing with its petty intrigues and constant positioning for funding and support. She joined the *Nightingale* to escape embarrassment and become a heroic explorer who could return to the First System in triumph. But return to what? Endless conferences and commerce squabbles?

Although she would not have admitted it a season ago, she was happier exploring the Thirteenth System than she had been in years. Of course, a day free of Lt. Clarence's sniping and incompetence was practically a holiday.

She wondered if it was worth the effort to petition for Clarence's replacement. Her last attempt was ignored, and it would have been easy to replace him while they were undergoing repairs on Fortuna. Now, he would need to be sent back with one of the militia patrols guarding the system's boundaries. While the *Nightingale* was designed to spend months in the stellar expanse, militia vessels needed to resupply every six to eight sevendays.

Mayhap Bran could be convinced. He was reasonable, and she could not completely fault his hostility toward Matahorn. Omar's malfeasance had left the free-trader systems to the mercy of pirates while extorting a fortune in import and export fees. For truth, other than Bran's free-trader background, she knew nothing to his discredit and had witnessed his courage, honor, and commitment to duty.

Getting to know him better and forging an understanding would be wise. She would like to tell herself that the anticipation and excitement she felt at the decision was due to the need to fulfill her duty, but she knew it was the warmth that flooded her senses in his presence. Her family would be horrified, but the Thirteenth System was a long way from the First. Matters were different here. She was a grown woman past forty capable of a liaison without losing her heart.

***

Sending a quick prayer to the Five Warriors, Bran activated the primitive beacon cobbled from salvaged communications parts. A soft chime confirmed it was broadcasting. The range was insufficient to reach the *Nightingale*, but flyers searching the plains would receive it. Now there was nothing to do but inventory the damage and wait.

He had at least two bells of light remaining and needed to make the most of it.

***

Adriana's eyes snapped open to a darkening sky. *Harpy scat.* She had dozed off. Her wrist tingled from the glowing alarm band. She had her specimens, and judging from the sun's position above the mountains, less than a period to take samples.

In the space of a few breaths, she was on the ground, snatching up the sample case. A quick calculation maximized her path. There was a chance the shadows from the forest would reach the final subject before Adriana did. If so, she would jettison the lure, releasing its contents to take cover.

She executed the first two harvests with ease, resisting her desire to watch the fluff balls scamper to safety. The third lure contained the same type of creature as the first, but there were variances within species that were worth exploring. More difficult was that it had become twisted in the plants. She could not leave it trapped, and disentangling it required more minutes than she had to spare.

Four and five went like clockwork. Racing for six, her foot caught in a hole and sent her sprawling. For long moments she lay in the heather, willing her lungs to work. Finally, gasping deep breaths, she found her knees and crawled the final few paces to her next subject.

It was new. With rabbitlike ears and the sinewy structure of a ferret, its mottled, dark blue fur blended into the shadows beneath the plants. When she pricked it for a sample, its eyes went from pink to gold, and fangs emerged. Fascinating.

She was tempted to keep it, but it would not serve. She had no reason to believe predator-rabbit would be immune to the unknown plague. Moving downwind four paces, she released it from the lure. Its snout lifted and it snarled before turning away. If it had caught her scent, it would have gone for Adriana.

Four lures remained, and the sun was touching the peaks. Risking a run, she reached the seventh and eighth lures.

The tenth was fully in shadow. Hoping the contents would have time to escape, she jettisoned it while sprinting to the ninth. Inside the lure, a round little fuzzball the size of her thumb pretended to be a seed pod from one of the blue trees.

It was adorable and fragile. She would need to be quick. Injector and extractor in hand, she reached in. "Come on little one." She tapped the extractor. It unfurled and accepted the tracker. "Well done, bella."

A flick of her finger collapsed the lure with a hiss. *Hiss?*

Adriana pivoted to the sound. *Rimon's dungeons!*

A forked tongue flickered between two-inch fangs, guided by cold, gray reptilian eyes. She grappled for her pistol knowing it was too late.

A snarling white blur hit the snake-thing and slammed it into the vegetation. Off balance, Adriana fell backward, still fumbling for her weapon. Digging in her heels, she scrabbled away from the growls and hisses of battle.

Sudden silence was more terrifying than the earlier sounds. Prey never heard their predators.

Finding her knees, she held the weapon ready, prepared to slay whatever predator had come out the victor.

A shaft of waning sunlight lit up bright blue eyes in a fuzzy white face. Braced on four equally fuzzy white feet, one planted on the dead snake, the serpent slayer wagged its tail.

***

Bran made a final note on this slate and closed the access panel. The saboteur had been thorough. It would be a day's work to get the DOP-C launch worthy. The cabin had dimmed while he had worked, without any sign of a flyer. Raleigh would continue sending searchers, but it could be the next day before they were found.

He and Adriana should secure the transport for the night.

Adriana?

Cyclops turds. The sun was almost down, and she had not returned. Bounding away from the console, he reached the weapons locker and the fireburst rifle.

***

It is impossible. It was right in front her, its wiry white coat gleaming in the fading light. Fourteen or fifteen inches from paw to crown, with a lot of height in its legs. It was maybe a stone in weight. Its narrow face was topped with triangular perked ears that were a bit large for its head. If not for the eye color, ears, and total lack of markings, it could be a rodent-hunting terrier from any number of systems. Taking a deep breath, Adriana lowered her weapon and held out a hand palm down, fingers curled.

The terrier, or terrier offshoot, cocked its head. It considered her ... her fingers ... then stepped forward. Taking another hesitant step, it sniffed, then huffed, before pushing its head under her fingers and into the palm of her hand.

With a gentle touch, she stroked behind its ears. Its happy sound emboldened her to scratch. It pushed harder into her hand, demanding more.

It is impossible—domesticated behavior from what has to be a wild a dog. But it is happening. The little creature had not taken its kill and retreated. Instead, it encouraged her contact. In the dimming light she looked into the intelligent blue eyes and voiced her thought, "Why?"

The tail wagged harder.

"Thank you, mighty warrior, for the rescue." She looked at the dead snake and itched to collect it. "Enjoy your meal."

The terrier-like creature whined, and nudged the snake in her direction. If it was offering . . . she pulled the collection device from her kit and hovered it over the snake. The terrier barked a domesticated canine bark.

Second Warrior protect me; the snake-thing is huge. Coiled in a sealed sample sack, it filled the case. She had to move the last of her sampling and tracking devices into the lures' case. The terrier yipped and turned in circles. It was adorable and she hated to leave it, but the darkness was spreading. There were far more deadly predators than that snake-thing in the forest. "I have to go."

Turning for the DOP-C, she spotted Bran standing on top—annoyance, if not outright anger, in every line of his frame. Had he said something about only a few paces? Glancing at her rescuer, she said, "I am in trouble."

Pulling the cases higher on her shoulder, she broke into a jog. Any faster and she might end up breaking an ankle in the next hidden hole. Within three strides, she realized Bran had the distance-viewer turned in her direction and was holding the fireburst rifle at his side, watching for predators. Her heart lifted. He might be angry, but he would protect her.

Another ten paces and she could make out his glower. No question she was in deep trouble.

Three more paces out, she called, "I can explain—"

"Keep running."

She knew those clipped tones. She had heard them for two days while they battled the despoiler fleet. The man was all soldier. All commander.

Reaching the DOP-C, she called, "I got it all and more."

The viewer dropped to hang around his neck. The fireburst rifle lifted. "Do not move."

Her heart shuddered and breath caught. What awful monster had followed her?"

A *yip* sounded.

She spun on her heels, throwing herself over the terrier. "Do not harm it."

***

The woman was deranged. Bran could find no other explanation. "It is not a terrier. It is not domesticated. That is impossible."

"It saved my life. It followed me home." Adriana shook her head as if attempting to clear cluttered thoughts. She shifted her shoulders, swinging both her sample cases behind her back. "If little blue eyes will come to me, I want a closer look."

"You named it?"

"What? No. It is but a description." She crouched before what he had to admit looked like a white, fox-sized terrier. With glowing blue eyes. Terriers did not have blue eyes. The weird creature tilted its head in one direction and then the other. It crouched, waggling its butt.

At Adriana's encouraging coo, it crawled into her arms. Murmuring endearments, she cuddled it close. "Blue eyes is a female. Her fur is softer than it looks."

"Wondrous. Now put it down and come inside."

She ignored him, checking the creature's ears. "Will you hand me the medic's scanner? I want to take some readings."

"No. This is ridiculous. Sample the thing and get in here. We need to seal up if we are going to keep the night insects at bay."

Sending him a furious glare, she reached into one of her cases and extracted a couple of instruments. The terrier-thing did not seem the least distressed at being stuck. It was not until Adriana put it down that it started to whine. The whine turned to an anxious bark as she scaled the side of the DOP-C.

Turning, she made a shooing motion. "Go on. Go back to your pack."

Following her into the DOP-C, Bran sealed the door closed. "I thought for a minute you were going to bring that thing inside."

She set her equipment cases beneath the storage compartments and rolled her shoulders. "I wanted to, but I cannot bring live samples onto the *Nightingale* until I discover what in the environment is toxic to them. And blue eyes did save my life." She opened a case and pulled out a large, sealed sample. "This thing is venomous, and I doubt there anything in the medic kit that could counteract it, assuming I survived long enough to make it back."

Even curled like a cargo line, Bran could tell the snake was at least three feet long and almost as thick as Adriana's wrist. The rectangular head displayed two-inch fangs. Gray diamonds marked its otherwise black skin. The chilling sight ratcheted his anger to a new level. "Nocturnal?"

"I think so." She closed the case. "If it came out in daylight, we would have encountered it before now."

Extracting two water vials from storage, he tossed her one.

With a grateful smile, she cracked the seal.

He waited until she had swallowed half before speaking. "Are you deranged? Incapable of following orders? You should never have been out there when the nocturnal creatures emerged."

Her eyes widened and a blush darkened her cheeks. "I apologize. I fell asleep while waiting for the lures to activate." Her sharp little chin came up. "I did jettison the sample closest to the forest."

"Closest to the forest? There was one even farther away from the DOP-C?"

She had the grace to look abashed. "Er, yes." But then that chin came up, again. "The breeze carried the lures a good distance. I did not have time to recast. It takes at least a bell for my scent to dissipate."

She fell asleep. The breeze carried the lures. Terror-fueled anger had him barking, "You are completely lacking in discipline. You endangered your life. The mission."

"I did apologize."

Bran clenched his fists against the desire to shake her. "This is your last landing until you can demonstrate the ability to follow orders."

"What? No." All signs of contrition vanished, replaced by defiance. "You cannot. I am the lead zoologist. We will not finish in time if I am confined to the *Nightingale*."

Bran's control snapped. His hands wrapped around her shoulders. So fragile. So readily slain. "You could have died."

Defiance fled as quickly as it had surfaced. Her dark eyes filled with remorse, and warm fingers pressed against his wrist. "I am sorry. I was foolish and I know it. You can have no notion how relieved I was when I saw you standing on top of the DOP-C with the rifle."

"Promise me you will not be so foolish, again." He squeezed her shoulders. "Your word."

With a deep breath she nodded. "My word."

She was in his arms, her head against his chest. Her black curls soft and springy under his lips. The pleasant scent of the purple flora tickled his nose. Bran enjoyed women, but none had felt so right in years. Not since he lost his wife in the pirate actions. The memory returned him to the present and the fact that he did not have her consent. With reluctance, he released her. "I overstep."

Her fingers lingered on his waist. "I do not object."

"This is not the best timing."

"I suppose not." With a sigh, she released him. "What of communications?"

"I managed to rig a beacon from the working equipment. We are close enough to our original destination that they will find us within a day. Mayhap by morning." He pulled a handful of nutrition bars from storage. "I will need to stay with the DOP-C until they return with replacement equipment, but you can return to the *Nightingale*."

Taking a bar, she tore open the wrapper. "Why? Another day will allow me to collect more samples. I can start at sunup. There will be no risk of another incident."

Dropping down on the bedding, he leaned back. "We can discuss it in the morning."

Joining him, she handed him a water vial. "Please. I did give my word. Blue eyes and the snake are evidence that there is far more to discover than we realized. It may be this section of forest or the proximity to the mountains."

"You are relentless." He bit into a bar.

"I am a scientist. Tenacity is a given." She popped a bite into her mouth.

He should insist she leave, but after nearly losing her twice in one day, he wanted her close.

Swallowing, she sighed. "I wish I could have spent more time examining blue eyes. She is a total enigma."

"How so?"

"White? It stands out like a beacon. Prey should see her coming and predators can track her with ease."

He swallowed the last of his bar and grabbed another. "It followed you without strain. Could it be fast enough to hunt and avoid being hunted?"

"Mayhap. She was a blur when she went for the snake. I had no idea what she was until the battle was over." She tore open another bar. "But that is not the only anomaly. She should have grabbed her kill and run. Or at the very least, snarled to warn me away. Instead, she wagged her tail. She accepted handling. That is domesticated behavior, and it is impossible. We are the first people to set foot on this planet in at least a thousand years."

3. Hidden Depths

Sevenday 31, Day 6

Adriana woke sore and groggy. She had slept soundly, but for too few bells. Ever since the samples succumbed to the unknown plague, her slumber had been disturbed. If she managed three bells at a stretch before agitated half-dreams pulled her awake, it was by the grace of the Five Warriors. She was so comfortable she might even sleep some more. Relishing Bran's masculine scent, she closed her eyes.

Bran? Last night they had lain side by side. Not touching. The wall that had become the floor was wide enough to spread the bedding, but the irregular surface created by the windows was like lying on rocks. Only by keeping the bedding stacked could they sleep.

It was practical. Except, she was half sprawled on the free-trader. Her head and torso rested on his chest, one leg between his thighs and one arm was wrapped around his waist.

Had she slept so comfortably when she was consort to Evander? *Do not go there.* That was the past. The present was duty and adventure. And the wonderful scent of her free-trader. For a few more moments, while he slept, she would enjoy their proximity.

***

Bran woke, fully alert, when the dawn brightened the windows over his head. It had always been so unless he was injured or ill. Even within the *Nightingale's* artificial day, he recognized dawn. He also recognized the scent of the woman cuddled against him. Adriana.

She had fascinated him from their first meeting. The Serengeti dossier held an impressive list of credentials. She had won awards for unearthing an ancients' technique for genetic filtering that enabled plains-dwelling grazers to thrive in the arid mountains of Socraide Deuce. That breakthrough catapulted her to the top of the Matahorn zoology department. It also introduced her to the lackluster warrior who took Adriana as consort.

The man was everything Bran despised about the warrior class: selfish, pretentious, and entitled. When the man managed to seduce the signet heir of a Matahorn supplier, he dissolved his contract with Adriana on less than a sevenday's notice.

Scum-sucking cyclops.

Adriana stirred. Her even breathing hitched. She was awake. Bran held in a sigh, wanting the moment to last. With a contented sound, she curled closer and returned to sleep.

***

Adriana's father squeezed her shoulder, gave her a gentle shake. Time to rise for school. Not school. *Nightingale.* Thirteenth System. Bright Star Deuce. Her eyes opened to a broad expanse of uniform gray. Bran's tunic. Bran's chest.

The gentle hand on her shoulder squeezed. "Wake. The day advances and I heard a flyer."

She lifted her eyes to see his gentle smile, his lips close enough to kiss. *Five Warriors take it.* Adriana rolled off Bran, feeling heat rising in her cheeks. She remembered her brief waking and then curling up close to her free-trader to enjoy more slumber. *Her* free-trader? Rising to her knees, she scrubbed her face with her hands.

Bran grinned. "Rise and shine, sleepy one. I think a flyer is inbound."

***

It was at least a bell past dawn, the sky a bright blue above the open door. Following Bran's example, Ariana snapped the lightweight blanket flat and attempted to roll it into a tight cylinder. "Why do DOP-C's have basic camping equipment?"

"Their purpose is to take shipments from stellar craft to planet surface. While most settlements have some form of guesthouse, they can be ... primitive. Sometimes, camping is better."

The blanket slid into its case with unexpected ease. "I thought you dropped supplies and returned."

Bran collapsed the first stacked camp bed. "It depends on the run and if we are collecting cargo."

Mimicking him, she collapsed the second. "I find it hard to imagine planets with so few stellar launch centers."

"Critical components could only be imported through the Matahorn supply depots. Only our largest cities had sufficient funds."

"I concede the supply depot fees were excessive." There was some justice to his complaint, but he fixated on the ill. "But the DOP-Cs would not exist if stellar launch centers were economical."

He snorted.

"Scoff all you like." She pushed the collapsed bedding into the storage compartment. "You and Raleigh are proud of your free-trader societies, and inventions like the DOP-Cs are going to catapult your Phoenix Enterprises to cartel status in a matter of decades."

Bran hesitated and then sealed the compartment. "Our inventiveness does not mitigate Matahorn greed."

There was no heat in the mechanical response.

She laughed. "How often have you rehearsed that line?"

He jerked his gaze to hers, surprise and chagrin in his expression. He shook his head. "We should tend to our biological imperatives before the flyer lands."

"Changing the subject?" She smiled, shaking her head. "I will take that as a concession."

His lips twitched and then a smile exploded with a deep chuckle. "Woman, you are impossible."

Failing to contain her own smile, she said, "I am brilliant and tenacious. Impossible is a side effect."

He tilted his head, eyes narrowed. "Are you flirting with me?"

Am I? "I believe I am."

"Good." He closed the distance between them, his fingers lifting her chin. "Then I am not misreading your interest."

Anticipation and desire unfurled. "Not in the least."

His lips were warm, the kiss gentle and all too brief. She opened her eyes to meet his amber gaze, his expression one of promise. Releasing her chin, he traced her jaw. "I would there were more time."

"That flyer will land any moment."

Regret flickered across his face as he turned to the storage compartments. Together, they gathered what they needed.

***

The mountain tips glowed in the early light. Adriana tied their freshening supplies to the end of the cargo line and dropped the satchel over the side. A thump behind her announced Bran emerging with the rifle. To their knowledge, the local predators were nocturnal, but Bran was not taking risks.

He settled with his back to her and the rope. "Talk to me while you are about your business. If you go silent, I will assume the worst."

It was a reasonable precaution, if awkward. Reaching the ground, she picked up the case and small spade. Two steps from the DOP-C, she noticed the purple plants moving against the breeze. She stepped backward toward the rope, raising the spade. "Bran?"

His boots thumped against the DOP-C. "Adriana?"

A bright patch of white appeared in the purple. "Blue Eyes?"

Bran's voice came from overhead, "What say you?"

"It is Blue Eyes." Dropping the spade, she crouched down for the terrier, unaccountably thrilled at the little creature's arrival. "What are you doing here?"

Tail wagging, the terrier looked up at her with a doggy grin. Unable to resist, she rubbed its ears, eliciting a happy moan. "Were you here all night? You must be thirsty."

Pulling a vial from a pocket, she poured water into a cupped hand. After a tentative sniff, a pink tongue emerged to slurp the offering.

Bran's voice was sharp. "What are you doing? You cannot feed that thing."

"Of course not. I could accidentally poison her. But, so far, all the mammals drink water, and what comes out of the *Nightingale* distilleries is microbe and toxin free."

"That is not my point."

Ignoring Bran, she poured the rest of the vial into her hand. "Blue seems determined to stay close."

"And when we leave?"

"She will have no reason to remain."

***

Bran used the distance-viewer to track the flyer's progress as it descended over the mountains. The graceful craft was half the size of the DOP-C, and most of that was propulsion. Fast and maneuverable, they had been invaluable in the battle for the Thirteenth System and were essential to the surveying and mapping of both habitable planets. Within breaths, the black fleck became a deep-scarlet flyer.

The color came from the special alloy used in the *Nightingale*'s hull and that of its flyers. Lightweight, it was more resistant to damage than standard hull alloys, deflecting not only stellar debris, but as it turned out, fireburst from attacking cannons.

Adriana said, "I thought the captain would send one of the Serengeti flyers."

Of the twelve *Nightingale* flyers that reached the Thirteenth System, only half survived the battle. Of the five Serengeti flyers that survived the destruction of the flagship, two had remained in the Thirteenth System. Almost as fast and maneuverable as *Nightingale* flyers, they were the standard blade-metal gray. Without the extensive survey training provided to the *Nightingale* pilots, they were the first deployed for search and rescue.

Bran lowered the viewer. "I expect that it is Nickolas. He was due to survey this grid within the sevenday. This way, he can collect preliminary data. He does not voice it, but feels he failed Serengeti by not discovering vistrite on Bright Star Prime."

Discovering vistrite would earn the entire crew magnificent bonuses as well as recognition. "None of the last six systems discovered held vistrite. Why would Nickolas feel he had a special obligation to discover it in the Thirteenth?"

Bran slanted her a glance. "Have you an understanding of geology?"

"It is limited. Why?"

"Metricelli Prime's planetary crust ranges in depth from five to forty-seven miles. The Great Crevasse is located where the crust is densest."

"It is thirty miles in depth now. How much deeper can it go?"

"I am not within crevasse security-privilege, but I cannot imagine more than another ten miles, assuming the vistrite goes that deep."

Adriana frowned. "It has been in use for well over a millennium. At that rate, we have at least a few centuries to discover a replacement."

"Vistrite demand is ten times what it was when the Sixth System and its vistrite deposit was discovered. It has doubled in the past two decades. Mercium is not only a cheap alternative in simple technology—it is essential to extending the vistrite horizon."

Her expression turned skeptical. "Every schoolchild knows that the vistrite supply will last at least another millennium."

"Forecasts beyond a decade or two are subject to wide variations. And a millennium is a nice round number. One that is far enough in the future to be meaningless."

Her eyes narrowed with a sharp inhale. "A fifty percent variation would not be impossible. The supply that might last only five hundred years and the last vistrite discovery eight centuries gone." She lifted her gaze. "Five Warriors protect us."

Bran gestured to the flyer preparing to land. "That warrior is a true follower of the Five Warriors. He believes he is honor bound to protect the Thirteen Systems from the forces of anarchy, and there is naught that would cause more anarchy than a vistrite shortage."

The brilliant scarlet flyer descended in a graceful glide six or seven paces west.

"He picked a good landing site." Adriana nodded. "Adjacent to our crash damage, it will limit disruption to the local ecological systems."

"That was not the purpose." Bran passed her the rifle and grabbed the line to descend. "The flyer needs to be on that side to pull the DOP-C back into position."

When Bran reached the flyer, the younger man had emerged. In his early thirties, Lieutenant Nickolas Cyncad was intelligent, well-trained and embodied everything a warrior was supposed to be and so few were: honorable, courageous, and dedicated to his duty. An inch or so taller than Bran, the flyer pilot was well-muscled and fit.

Nickolas reached out to grab Bran's forearm. "Well met."

Bran returned the clasp. "Well met indeed."

Nickolas' assessing gaze went to the woman standing guard on the DOP-C. "Was this another bout of fabricated ill luck?"

Raleigh had ordered Bran to keep quiet about his suspicions, but Nickolas was one of the few crew members they trusted implicitly. When they had unmasked the original *Nightingale* captain as the pirate Sadico, Nickolas had fought at their side. "What are you asking?"

Nickolas' eyes did not leave Adriana. "I do not need to be an expert in complexity theory to recognize when too much coincidence means a pattern. When I approached the captain, he admitted you both share my suspicions. So, is this part of the pattern?"

It was a relief to have Nickolas included. "Whoever it is, their success has made them arrogant. I helped design the DOP-C. Tampering would not escape my notice."

Nickolas' mouth hardened to a grim line. "The Serengeti replacement pilot originally scheduled for the flight does not have your skill."

Cyclops piss. If the DOP-C had fallen at the first propulsion failure, passengers and craft would have been obliterated.

Adriana was watching them. Nickolas reached into the flyer. "Any idea why someone wants Lt. Commander Adriana dead?"

"The loss of a pilot and zoology lead would further slow progress."

Nickolas pulled out a coil of alloy line. "Could be another Matahorn intrigue. If we fall far enough off schedule, Monsignor Horatio might convince Leonardo to switch its allegiance from Serengeti."

Bran's blood chilled. The wily Matahorn preeminence led the first among cartels and controlled a significant voting bloc in the governing council. He had not gained and held power for three decades without being ruthless. "Taking out the Matahorn lead scientist does divert suspicion."

Nickolas handed Bran the fasteners. "In one sense, the captain is pleased. At least we can strike her from the list of possible saboteurs."

***

Adriana sat behind Nickolas as he started the flyer, the whine of the propulsion system muted by the cabin. Fifteen paces beyond, Bran stood waiting. Nickolas taped the console. The flyer did not move. Another tap. It lurched and then began to roll.

The craft was designed for flight, not the plains' uneven surface. Nickolas' fingers moved in an erratic pattern, keeping the craft in motion but on the ground. They drew closer to Bran. The flyer shuddered. Glancing at a display panel, she could see the DOP-C rock.

Nickolas stroked the console. "Come on darling. You can do it."

Apparently, it was not only freighter pilots who seduced their craft. The flyer lurched forward, and the DOP-C tumbled. Both Bran's hands came up at the same moment Nickolas cut the power.

Nickolas turned with a grin. "That should do it. Let us go inspect the damage."

The drop from the flyer to the ground was not far, but with his typical courtesy, Nickolas reached up to assist her. She rather liked him, but then most people did. He was particularly popular with the female crew both for this pleasant manner and handsome face. With green eyes, auburn hair, and chiseled features, he could have starred in holographic entertainments instead of hazarding his life in an uncharted section of the galaxy.

He was also modest, never mentioning his close ties with Monsignor Lucius and the monsignor's legendary consort, Lilian Thornraven. After the Serengeti flagship was destroyed in battle, the couple took up residence on the *Nightingale*. It did not require a scientist's skills in observation to notice the respect and affection between them and Nickolas. And yet, like Bran who was also on familiar terms with the duo, the lieutenant never referenced his powerful connections.

If Clarence were the same caliber as Nickolas, Adriana's life would be far more pleasant. Unlike Nickolas, her Serengeti assistant never lost an opportunity to remind her that he was a warrior of Serengeti while she was a commoner of Matahorn. Nor did Nickolas appear to resent taking orders from Bran, a commoner and free-trader. Had Clarence's constant harassment prejudiced Adriana against the Serengeti?

Bran's frown jolted her from her thoughts. "Bran, what is amiss?"

He blinked, his expression clearing. "With luck, nothing." He clapped Nickolas' shoulder. "I have an inventory of what is needed to repair the internal workings. Let us see if there is any external damage on the side that hit the ground."

Nickolas nodded, his gaze drifting toward the mountains. "It is odd, but there is something familiar about that range."

Bran shrugged. "You surveyed two on Prime and one other here on Deuce."

"But there is something. Mayhap, I should swing south and trace more of that range."

Bran shook his head. "Better to keep to the designated grid order. It is too easy to miss a few important miles by veering off. Your schedule brings you back within the sevenday. Those mountains are not going anywhere."

With one last look at the mountains, Nickolas followed Bran. Slowing her pace, Adriana took a moment to enjoy the sight of Bran walking away. He moved with a more concentrated energy than Nickolas, and while there was no denying the younger man's appeal, he did not stir warmth in her the way Bran did. There was a solidity to Bran. The certitude that came from forging his own destiny.

Lost in her musings, she was three paces back. Hastening her pace, she caught the last of Nickolas' comment.

". . . Raleigh or me. It is unlikely the saboteur is in the command crew, but—" Nickolas broke off as she reached them.

Saboteur. She had wondered, but it seemed so unlikely. "You think sabotage? But all the crew and replacements were double-checked for despoiler affiliations after the battle."

Nickolas exchanged a glance with Bran that seemed to be an entire conversation. At Bran's nod, he said, "The despoilers were not the only source of intrigue in the Thirteen Systems. You know as well as we do that every position on the *Nightingale* was negotiated among the three partners. The alliance is fragile at best."

"Well, you cannot suspect Matahorn. After the command crew, I am the highest-ranking member of the group."

Bran's soft tone belied his frown. "Do you really believe that Monsignor Horatio is above sacrificing one of his retainers to achieve his ambitions? One who is not even a warrior?"

The warrior who had taken Adriana consort had no such qualms. *No.* She would not be deflected. "And, of course, you assume it could not be Serengeti. Monsignor Lucius is in no way ruthless."

Instead of being offended, Nickolas laughed. "Monsignor is beyond ruthless." He sobered. "But Monsignor is in no manner callous. He would not instigate actions that could cause your death or any of the crew for some marginal advantage in Bright Star. And that is all it would be."

Bran added, "Do not underestimate Captain Raleigh's shrewdness. Other than Nickolas, he is no more certain of Serengeti than any others. Jarrod was a Serengeti selection."

"Captain Jarrod? He was hero."

"He was despoiler and almost hijacked the *Nightingale* before she launched."

What says he? Blood thundered in her ears. It could not be true. "The media. Monsignor Horatio."

Bran's hand rested on her shoulder. "The truth about Jarrod was hidden because neither Serengeti nor Matahorn wanted to reveal they knew the despoilers were rising. Now that they have been defeated, it is no longer a secret."

As if sensing Adriana's legs had turned liquid, Bran's arm went to her waist. "Let us continue this inside."

Seated in the DOP-C, Adriana looked from one man to the other. "You truly believe someone is sabotaging our mission and it is a routine commerce intrigue?"

They both nodded.

She sat back. "I am no longer a suspect because I could have died in the crash?"

More nods. As much as she would like to deny it, the pieces fit. "What do we do?"

Nickolas flashed a grin. "You are taking this very well."

"I am a scientist. Disliking an answer does not change it. Altering the constraints or variables might." She turned to Bran. "What do we do?"

Approval glowed in his eyes as he leaned forward. "Continue the pretense we believe it ill luck, or hasty repairs on Fortuna after the battle when all was in disarray, or any reasonable explanation that does not include sabotage."

"Captain Raleigh does not wish to alert the saboteur."

"Exactly," Nickolas replied. "They might cease, and we need to identify them, and more importantly, who is behind all this."

"There is more to it," Bran said. "Since the battle, tension has remained high. Any suggestion of sabotage could have the crew turning on each other and that could do far more damage."

***

Bran watched the flyer disappear into the clouds. Nickolas had raised an eyebrow when informed Adriana would remain with Bran but said nothing, merely relaying Bran's requirements to the *Nightingale*. Another flyer would arrive within two bells with the needed parts. Fortunately, the side of the DOP-C that had hit the ground was scraped and dented but sound.

Next to him, Adriana sighed.

He glanced at her. "Regretting your decision to remain?"

It would be at least the following day before he had the damaged systems repaired and the DOP-C flight worthy.

"No, regretting we did not think to ask for additional food supplies along with the replacement parts. And I would love a cup of tea, or even the bitter Fortuna kaffee."

He glanced at the endless plains of inedible plants. "Are there ground squirrels in this area?"

Twice the size of squirrels, the local animals were burrowers, but had a distinctive fluffy tail that gave them their name. They were among the few local fauna that had been cleared for consumption.

"I have not seen any, but the conditions are right." Adriana shot him a quizzical look. "Have you means and skill to cook it?"

"Of course; I can dress it, too."

"Good. My food preparation skills are limited to a proper cooker." She turned for the DOP-C. "Not that I can promise ground squirrel, but I will know to harvest it if one enters a lure."

He could not hide his surprise. "You can cook?"

"Why are you surprised?"

"Few of your status bother to learn."

She reached into the compartment for her equipment. "I am not quite the pampered First System dweller you believe."

Is my opinion so obvious?

She glanced up at him and laughed. "I am well aware of how free-traders view First System dwellers. It is even justified to an extent." She pulled out a case. "I am not a fan of the processed meals that are standard fare in field expeditions. It was either learn to cook what I liked or live on raw vegetables."

She was proving more intriguing with each bell. Reaching down, he grabbed a case and carried it to the entrance. "You are astonishing."

She threw him a surprised look. "Are you flirting?"

Is he? "Mayhap. It is not an area where I have much practice."

Her lips curved. A teasing sparkle entered her eyes. "It is difficult to flirt with three-word sentences. Although you did well with that last."

"Am I so taciturn?"

She shook her head, setting a case by the door. "At first. Not so much anymore. Stellar exploration seems to have mellowed you."

"That is not it." He closed the distance. "I filter less when I am with someone I know and like."

Her eyes widened, and color deepened on her cheeks. "Oh. I like you. Too."

Her confusion was adorable and gratifying. "Now who is using three-word sentences?"

She shook her head. "What is it about you that returns me to my awkward twenties?"

He cupped her cheek, relishing the velvety softness. "You are a compelling woman." He yielded to temptation and feathered a kiss across her lips. "I wish our circumstances were better."

Her smile turned wry. "They are better than yesterday. At least we have a working freshener."

A laugh escaped him. "And a great deal of work to do."

Grabbing the distance-viewer, she turned for the doorway.

Reaching it, she glanced back. "We can practice your flirting when the sun goes down."

***

Sitting in the doorway, Adriana used the distance-viewer to examine the mountain range. Bringing the mountains 10,000 feet closer did not add much detail but did give a hint of the beige grasslands that took over from the plains in another ten miles or so. Whatever had caught Nickolas' attention would remain a mystery for a few more days.

Behind her, Bran made occasional grunts as he worked to remove the damaged system parts.

Turning her attention to the forest, she found the viewer far more useful. The nearest edge was not more than two hundred paces. Close enough that Bran's caution was warranted. There were feline-type predators that were remarkable sprinters and could reach the DOP-C in a matter of breaths. With the sun nearing its peak, the area at the edge was shady but not dark. She could make out individual trunks and pale-pink fernlike plants that clustered near the red deciduous trees.

Bran snorted. "Scum-sucking cyclops."

She turned into the vehicle. "What is a cyclops?"

Bran made an interrogative sound, his head emerging from the open hatch in the floor. "What say you?"

"I asked, what is a cyclops? You have referenced its turd, piss, and scum-sucking since the crash."

He blinked. Color warmed his cheeks and a rueful smile formed. "I was unaware. A cyclops is a rodent that inhabits the caverns in the eastern part of Redemption. They are almost the size of that terrier you found, only not as charming. The color of pus, they have one eye, two sets of sharp teeth, and reek of the carrion that makes up their diet."

"Lovely. In the First System there are harpies. Nasty winged things that like to nest on the city spires and eat garbage."

His smile turned into a chuckle. "I thought you were going to set more lures."

"I am." Standing, she let the viewer drop to hang by its strap and grabbed her cases. "I am going to the west. I do not think we are close enough to the mountains to see any variations in fauna, but it is worth checking. I will need to go past where the flyer landed, so it will be a while."

It was a beautiful day; bright, temperate and with a light breeze. She hoped Blue was all right. She was not sure when, but somewhere along the way, the description "little blue eyes" had become the name Blue. The little creature had disappeared sometime during Nickolas' landing, and she had not seen it since. She had half hoped Blue would return while she was scanning the area. Poor thing. All these strange metal birds dropping from the sky must be traumatic.

Three paces past the landing area, Adriana began casting the lures in a wide arc. Despite the challenging circumstances, she was in a bright mood. She knew it was that brief kiss. That was more than flirting. As much as she wanted to believe the attraction she felt was mutual, it had seemed unlikely. The visual of his deceased wife showed a tall, willowy woman with pale patrician features and elegant waves of dark honey hair. Physically, she could not be more different from Adriana. An artist of some renown in the free-trader systems, her temperament would have been nothing like Adriana's analytical responses. And yet, Bran had kissed her. Twice. However briefly.

She dropped the final lure within six paces of the tree line and the promising pink ferns. Pulling the viewer, she confirmed her hope: slender yellow stalks of peach-berries nestled among the fronds. Named for their color and fuzzed skin, the egg-sized berries tasted more like plum and had become a crew favorite.

Standing there, the lure case empty, Adriana was torn. She promised Bran she would not take foolish chances. With the sun high up, was it foolish to take those last few steps? She unholstered the fireburst pistol. She *was* armed. Not that it helped with the snake.

A yip from the right snapped her attention away from the trees. Blue stood a pace away, her head cocked to one side and tail in a slow wag.

"Did you come to help? What do you think? Will Bran agree that between you and the pistol I am sufficiently cautious?"

She looked over at the tempting fruit.

The tip of Blue's muzzle lifted, and delicate muscles fluttered as she took in the scents of the area. Her lips curled and, with a sharp bark, she leapt away from the trees. Adjusting the cases on her shoulder, Adriana followed. If there was something in those trees Blue wished to avoid, Adriana wanted no part of it.

The terrier glanced back and, seeing Adriana follow, gave a happy prance. Checking the wind, Adriana veered east, away from the latest set of lures, taking an oblique angle back to the DOP-C. Blue yipped and moved in the other direction.

Odd. If Blue wanted to raid the lures, she should instinctively stay downwind. "Sorry Blue, I need to go this way."

With a disgruntled sound, Blue abandoned her course to accompany Adriana. Did the dog understand Adriana's words or simply accept that Adriana had a different agenda? Growing up, her parents had dogs. Bred for hunting, they enjoyed her father's hikes when he went on his insect-hunting expeditions. He always claimed that the dogs understood more than he imagined and less than he would wish.

By the time they reached the DOP-C, Adriana's bracelet had pinged two alerts.

***

After double-checking the connections, Bran pushed off his knees, arching his back to stretch out the kinks. Leaving the floor panel open, he reached for a water vial. He was glad of the temperate day. The environmental controls were undamaged, but he had powered off all the systems while he worked to remove the damaged parts.

Outside, the clouds had cleared, leaving a cobalt-blue sky. The color reminded him of Adriana's stray. That was not a natural color for a dog's eyes. If it was a dog. Until they returned to the *Nightingale*, and Adriana evaluated her samples, they would not know.

The woman had accepted the revelations of sabotage and Jarrod's perfidy with remarkable aplomb. Her wariness of Serengeti was no worse than most of the Serengeti crew's wariness of Matahorn. Unfortunately, those attitudes colored not only opinions, but perceptions of events. It made the investigation far more difficult. In Adriana's favor, she was not blindly loyal to her cartel. She could and would entertain information that was not flattering to Matahorn or Horatio Margovian. That made her far less biased than most, and her observations more valuable.

The thought pleased him. As did her flirting and admission of attraction. He also wanted her to trust him fully. From her reactions this morning, she was close. Most of her initial wariness had faded over the months as her analytical mind weighed her observations against First System anti-Serengeti and anti-free-trader bias. He suspected that what little remained was the wariness they all felt after the battle with the despoilers.

The object of his musing spoke from the doorway. "Bran? Is all well?"

"I have pulled most of the damaged parts. What of your samples?"

"Two of the lures are active. It would be better to wait until more respond before collection. I was going to grab a nutrition bar while I waited."

Bran's stomach approved with a loud rumble. "If you grab the bars and water, I will lower a couple of passenger seats."

She climbed inside, setting her cases by the door. "Ah, I am not alone."

Two fluffy white paws were planted on the bottom of the doorframe. Two unnaturally blue eyes stared at him with expectation.

"She is back?"

Sidling past the opening in the floor, Adriana reached into storage for the bars and water. "She met me as I finished setting the lures."

Reaching across the hole, she handed him two bars and a water vial. "I need to give Blue some water."

Squatting by the door, she repeated the morning's water sharing. "You know that is ill-advised."

She sighed. "I know. But she has helped me twice."

"Twice?"

With a sheepish smile, Adriana fondled the dog's ears. "There were peach-berries."

As she continued, he was torn between laughter and fear. "Would you really have broken your word for some fruit?"

"Until Blue came along, I had decided that even with a pistol, it was too much risk. There are good reasons foraging groups have armed militia standing guard."

"You would have considered Blue equivalent to a militia guard?" *Cyclops piss.* When had he started calling the dog by name?

"It was more—did she think it safe? She lives here and can handle a massive snake." Ariana gave the creature one last pat before rising. "When she turned tail, that was the answer. Not safe."

She took the seat next to his and tore open a bar. "I doubt she understands what a fireburst pistol can do. But it was no help last night, so I would be foolish to rely on it."

Relieved the woman was both sensible and honorable, Bran tore into his bar. It was too bad about the peach-berries. Adriana was right, the nutrition bars were getting old.

Adriana's lips twitched. "Regretting the peach-berries?"

Had she read his mind? Probably his expression. "Emergency rations are life sustaining, but that is all that can be said for them."

Leaning back, she took a sip of water. "As a child, I found them exotic."

That made no sense. Adriana came from a wealthy family. "When did you have recourse to nutrition bars?"

"My father is an etymologist. He would take me on day trips to study insects. The nutrition bars were lunch." She broke off a small piece. "I was thinking about him earlier. He was no end of amused when I chose zoology. 'The perfect compromise between medic and bug collector.' He used to talk to our dogs, too. Said it was only a problem if he started hearing answers."

Enchanted at the image of a small Adriana chasing butterflies, he almost missed her last comment. "Talked to dogs, too? As you talk to the terrier?"

"You talk to the DOP-C, and it cannot actually hear you." She shrugged. "Blue responds to the sound of my voice. And probably my body language."

Common enough in domesticated animals, but less so in wild ones. He glanced out the door where Blue had flopped down in a patch of sun. It had not yet been a full day and Adriana was bonding with the thing. The longer they stayed, the worse it would get. A glance at the time showed it was later than he realized. "The flyer should be here with the parts. I wonder if—"

The distinct hum of a flyer broke in as if summoned.

Ariana stood, tossing her wrappers and vial in the recycler. "This is ill-timed. Only half the lures are filled, and the sound will chase everything out of the area for several bells."

"You will have time tomorrow. It will take half a day to install the new components."

"You will not work at night?"

"Cannot, rather. We will need environmental systems and I cannot make repairs with the power active."

***

"Almost . . . almost." Bran twisted his torso, straining for leverage on the resistant connection. The DOP-C was designed for ease of repair, the system components modular and readily exchanged. Whoever had sabotaged the DOP-C had managed to sever the connector to a vistrite controller, leaving a small section of the coupling connected to the DOP-C. Until Bran worked it free, he could not snap in the replacement part. Squeezing his hands into the tight space only increased the difficulty. "Almost."

The tool slipped, clanging against the bottom, the sudden loss in tension sending his knuckles barking against the unit. "Demon piss!"

Shaking his wounded hand, he fished around in the hole for the dropped tool.

Ariana's cool voice came from the doorway. "An escalation in expletives. That does not sound promising."

His fingers closed over the tool, and he rolled toward the door.

Adriana was a dark silhouette framed in light. The sun was still above the peaks, but they did not have much more than another period of daylight. "Were you successful?"

"Six new samples." She set her cases inside the door. "No luck on the ground squirrel."

Disappointment worsened his mood. "Our saboteur has a surprising knowledge of systems. They severed the coupling to the vistrite controller about two-thirds through. The strain of entry did the rest. It also left a jagged piece jammed into the housing. Until I remove it, I cannot replace the controller."

Her brow furrowed. "Controller couplings usually twist free."

"This one will, too. When I get a good grip on it."

Her eyes ran to his hands and then the opening in the floor. "Let me try."

"What say you?"

"I have assembled analytics equipment. I know how to lock in a controller. Or unlock it." She waved her hands in front of his face. "Mine are half the size of yours. A better fit."

He had the sudden desire to capture one of those hands and nip her fingers. *Now is not the time.* Throttling his libido, he moved away from the opening. Using the same gesture as if it were a blade, he offered the tool handle first, resting on his wrist.

"Ever the gallant officer." Her lips curved, and she accepted his offering. "And you managed to flirt without saying a word."

She was a delight. Smiling, he sat against the wall to watch her peer into the hole.

"I see it." She leaned in, bracing with her free hand. She made a series of questioning sounds, her luscious derriere wriggling in an appealing manner. A tsking sound followed. A bit more wriggling that sent his mind down a salacious path.

She stiffened. "Yes!"

Adriana pulled back, the tool raised in triumph, controller shard trapped in the clamp.

Unable to resist, he reached forward and pulled her into a hug. It was all too easy in their kneeling position for his hands to find her buttocks and caress their firm weight. With a sweet moan, her head tilted back, her lips grazing his.

Desire roared from his depths. He pressed her closer, deepening the kiss. Her lips parted, inviting him into the warm seductive cavern of her mouth. She was sweet and savory, his shaft hardening at the aphrodisiac.

Metal clanged on metal. He jerked away, seeking the threat. He took a shuddering breath when he realized she had dropped the mechanic's tool. He turned back to her, but she was already moving away.

Her eyes were huge, her cheeks flushed deep bronze, her lips dark and swollen. Running a hand through her curls, she shook her head. "Bran. I . . . Maybe. When we are back on the *Nightingale*."

"You are right. This is not the time or the place. But I will hold you to revisiting this once we are back on the *Nightingale*."

The confusion cleared, replaced by a shy smile. "I would like that."

***

The freshening packet was not a shower, but it did rid Adriana of two days' grime. She wished there was something similar for her uniform, or at least her socks and underthings. Donning soiled clothes against her freshly cleansed skin was not appealing. After a brief mental debate, she left off socks, trousers, and bra. A tunic and briefs were enough for sleep, and her legs were one of her better features.

There was more than enough mouth cleansing fluid to last through the next day. Mentally blessing the free-trader protocol that kept the DOP-Cs stocked with essentials, she washed away the nutrition bar residue.

With the new and damaged components filling a portion of the cargo area, there was only sufficient floor space for one set of bedding. The notion of sleeping curled against Bran was beyond appealing. And while the floor of a DOP-C was not ideal for shared pleasure, she would not object to more kissing. Combing her hair with her fingers, she accepted she was as presentable as she could be under the circumstances.

Bran's eyes widened and his appreciative gaze lingered on her legs. "Good notion. We will be more comfortable, and warm enough since we can use the blankets as intended and not as extra padding."

The camping bed was not as comfortable as the one in her *Nightingale* cabin, but it was a great deal more pleasant than the prior night's improvised version. Curled on her side, she could look out the window and up at the stars. Sinead's seer had marked out some of the constellations and she could make out the raven. Whether inspired by the Five Warriors or simply the seer's fancy, Adriana found it comforting to be able to find a familiar shape in the alien sky.

Below the single moon, two bright stars glittered, the blue-white color making her think of Blue's eyes. She hoped the little terrier had found a safe bed for the night. She had followed Adriana back to the DOP-C but disappeared while Adriana wrestled with the broken coupling.

The freshener opened. Bran was even more imposing from her position on the floor, the strong columns of his legs setting off little twinges of desire.

His voice held a hint of amusement. "Stargazing?"

Heat suffused her face, and she turned it back toward the raven. "We can see the raven. There are two stars close together that remind me of Blue's eyes. I was trying pick other stars to form a dog."

The bed shifted with his weight, and his warmth enveloped her with the arm he draped over her waist. "Show me."

***

The woman was a delight. He would never have suspected the driven scientist had such a fanciful side. The physical pull he had felt from the first was rapidly developing into something deeper and more profound.

". . . the tips of her ears." Adriana finished her star-drawing of Blue. "I think one of the geologists has some artistic talent. Maybe he will draw the constellation, if asked. I have several visuals of Blue."

"I am sure he will." Bran would make certain of it. Rolling to his back, he gave a gentle tug to pull her with him. "My other arm is falling asleep."

She settled against him with an embarrassed laugh. "I beg pardon. I do tend to get obsessed when I am working on a project."

"I noticed." It almost got her killed the evening gone. "Hazard of your career choice?"

"Or perhaps it is my nature and led to the choice. It comes at a cost."

The sorrow in her voice caught at his heart. "How so?"

The silence stretched and he thought she would not answer when she finally sighed. "If I had not been so obsessed with commerce advancement, I would have seen the dissolution of my consort alliance coming."

Is she deranged? "You cannot truly blame yourself. He was a fool to let you go."

She lifted her head, her dark eyes holding more resignation than pain. "I do not blame myself for the dissolution, only that I did not see it coming." She dropped her head back to his shoulder. "And for being lackwit enough to believe he loved me."

Bran had the overwhelming desire to rip the man's head from his shoulders. "You are a brilliant, intriguing, lovely woman. Why would you doubt a man's professed affection? One who was supposed to be an honorable warrior."

She shifted against him, one hand resting on his hip. "I was thirty-two and wooed by a Margovian Warrior. I was so dazzled that I abandoned my training. I did not observe, analyze, and then conclude. I wished him to be honorable and discarded any evidence that challenged my conclusion."

"Your family favored the match?"

"Of course they did. A warrior alliance? If I had borne a child, it would have been a warrior."

He felt her breath catch, more than heard it. "Did you wish a child?"

"Not immediately. My commerce career was taking off and the consort alliance pushed it even higher. It was five years before I seriously thought of conception. Evander would not agree. There was always a reason to wait another season."

Cyclops scat. "He was seeking another alliance."

"Our alliance had given him entrée into the serious commerce circles of Matahorn and the First System. He was, *is*, handsome, charming, of a good bloodline, and, due to my income, could afford to woo a signet heir."

"Your income?"

"Master research zoologists are compensated almost as well as junior seigneurs. His family stipend was less than mine, his artist income decent by commoner standards but paltry by warrior standards. But that was not my only value. As an artist he was not considered a warrior of substance. Having consort who was both a scientist and successful in commerce gave him weight."

"Why did you tolerate it?"

Her head lifted, shame marring her features. "I was a lackwit. I saw none of this until I was given notice of the alliance dissolution. But I spent as many bells at research as I do now. When I was at liberty, Evander kept us busy with social events and entertainments. And, on the few occasions when I felt something was off, he had a way of making me feel that I erred."

Cupping her face, he shook his head. "Evander is the lackwit. He had you and did not value you."

For a moment she appeared dubious, and then a tremulous smile emerged. "Other than the lack of a child, I am grateful he was a lackwit. Otherwise, I would not be on the *Nightingale*."

"Then I will be grateful as well." He wanted to claim a kiss, but not while her thoughts were on another man. "Have you always enjoyed stargazing? Is that what motivated you to join the *Nightingale*?"

Her nose crinkled. "I wish I could voice yes, but my interest in astronomy is incidental to my love of the sagas and entertainments about the discovery and founding of the Twelve Systems."

She is truly adorable. "Did you imagine yourself the intrepid captain guiding the stellar exploration vehicle through the beaconless expanse?"

"Sometimes." She settled against him. "Sometimes I was the sassy subordinate who kept them on their toes."

He swallowed his laughter lest it wound her. She could not be further from the often-shallow characters who were foils to the lead in those entertainments.

She raised her head, lips twisted in a wry smile. "It was a child's fantasy." Her expression turned curious. "What of you? Did being raised on freighters make planet life seem dull?"

"Quite the contrary. I loved the comfort of planet dwelling. I remember having my first bath at ten. It was beyond luxury to submerge in warm water."

"But you're a freighter pilot and navigator."

"My parents ran freight. Yours are scientists." He gazed at the sparkling sky, thinking about the past, at the decisions that brought him to this moment. "I do enjoy plotting a course between systems and visiting new places. But if I had not met Raleigh, I might have taken a different path."

She stroked his waist and made an encouraging sound.

"There were no funds for my advanced studies. What I learned about engineering came from the public archives and hands-on experimentation. Until I met Raleigh, no one with ownership in a freight enterprise would even look at my designs."

"I thought the free-trader systems were more open-minded."

"We are not as concerned about hereditary genetics as the other systems. Academic credentials are another matter. But Raleigh was ambitious and—with only three freighters—struggling to expand." He could still recall the excitement of joining Raleigh's Phoenix Enterprises. "He gave me a contract in return for access to my design for improved fuel efficiency. It was enough to give him the edge he needed."

"And then what?"

"His fleet expanded to twenty vessels and came up against the biggest competitors. The ones who had long-term contracts for most of the launch-pad pavilions. Unless the Eleventh and Twelfth Systems built more launch pads, we could expand no further."

Adriana rose on her elbow, eyes bright. "So, you invented the DOP-Cs?"

He could not suppress his grin. "Our first DOP-C was not much more than an automated glider with limited capacity and range, but it took us into untapped markets. It also gave Raleigh access to the planetary and system councils."

"And now he's a deacon, and this"—she gestured at the four-passenger transport—"is the third generation?"

At his nod, her smile warmed, and that teasing sparkle entered her eyes. "It seems my girlish fantasies were not so far off, except it is the brilliant and intrepid navigator who stirs my interest."

It was not the time or the place to indulge in passion, but he could not resist claiming a kiss.

4. Scientists and Sabotage

Sevenday 31, Day 7

Adriana half lifted her eyelids to the dim light. The sun was rising, the deep blue sky streaked with gold and lavender. One day, she would remember to ask the meteorologists about the causes of the sky tones, so different from the greens of Socraide Prime. She could feel Bran's warmth at her back, his sonorous breathing as comforting as his presence. Like most inhabitants of the Thirteen Systems, she did not confuse physical passion with love or commitment, but she had never been interested in it as mere recreation. She knew that her growing admiration and affection for Bran increased his physical appeal.

She wondered at her willingness to reveal so much to him. In part, it was that he trusted her with the secret of the *Nightingale* saboteur, but mostly because she felt safe with him. That he was Serengeti was awkward, but many couples navigated commerce conflicts. As for being a free-trader, she was coming to believe that First System attitudes about those systems might suffer from unfounded bias, or perhaps self-serving bias. What she knew for certain was that his admiration and passionate kisses eased wounds she had not realized still festered.

Bran's breathing changed and she felt him move. "Are you awake?"

Turning, she met his sleep-heavy eyes. "Yes."

He was oddly appealing with his hair tousled, his chin scruffy from two days' growth. He half smiled, a finger reaching to push a curl back from her forehead.

"Is my hair a wreck? Flat on one side, all odd angles on the other?"

His smile broadened. "It is rather adorable."

She was not certain what to make of that, but at least he was not repulsed.

His expression sobered. "Poor choice of compliment?"

"What say you?"

His forefinger touched the space between her brows. "Your dubious expression."

"Oh." She shook her head. "It is only that adorable seems an odd characteristic for a woman past her fortieth year."

He chuckled and sat up. "You will be adorable at eighty."

Flustered, she was saved from a response when he rolled from the mattress and rose. Holding out a hand, he said, "I need to finish the repairs. If all goes well, we will be ready to launch by midday."

Taking his hand, she scrambled to her feet. "Then I have time to set a handful of lures. It will make up for the ones that were empty, yesterday."

"Plan to return by midday."

Nodding her agreement, she hastened into the freshener. Her hair was as bad as she feared but she did not linger, knowing Bran needed the facility. By the time they had stowed the bedding and consumed a breakfast of nutrition bars, the sun was well up. Bran was lifting new parts from their crates when she grabbed her equipment cases.

Recessing the door, she scanned the area hoping for a patch of white. Her heart dropped when there was no sign of Blue. It was probably better. She was already too attached to the little creature. Shouldering her cases, she glanced back. Bran was bent over the open floor with a crate of replacement parts next to him. "I am off."

His head lifted. "Be careful."

She shifted her hip to display the pistol. "I will be fine."

"Midday."

"Midday," She agreed.

Her feet hit the ground to the sound of an unmistakable yip. Blue stood at the edge of the crushed area, tail waving in welcome.

"I am glad you are here, but this will be our final adventure."

The terrier's head cocked as if considering Adriana's words, and then, with a little bounce, she turned for the west.

"Not that way. It is south for us." Adriana shared Nickolas' curiosity about the mountain range, but south would provide a 360-degree sampling of the area around the DOP-C. Not a full grid, but a substantial piece of one. So far, she had replaced all but two of the lost samples, and—including Blue and the snake—identified four more. Whether she filled in the last of the destroyed samples, or found new varieties, the mission would be a success.

Adjusting the cases, she set the direction hoping Blue would follow. The little creature watched her in unmistakable doggy annoyance and then finally capitulated, bounding through the plants to catch up.

***

Bran ran the diagnostics a second time. Propulsion was operating within protocol. Navigation and communications were functional. He was confident he could get them back to the *Nightingale*, but he would want a thorough maintenance overhaul before letting the DOP-C make another flight. Changing the systems' status from maintenance to active, he closed the opening in the floor.

Adriana's voice came from the doorway. "This is good-bye."

She had set down her cases and crouched before the terrier, rubbing its ears. "I would take you with me if I could. But it is not safe for you."

The little dog made a happy moaning sound and pushed into Adriana. Bran could hear tears in her voice when she said, "I will miss you, too."

After a final pat, she stood and picked up her equipment. When she turned toward Bran, her face was tight, and her eyes held the sheen of unshed tears. His heart aching for her, he reached down to lift the cases. Knowing nothing he could say would make her feel better, he carried the cases back to the storage area. Deciding activity was the best course, he asked, "Will you stow everything while I run the prelaunch protocols?"

"Of course."

Settling in front of the console, he activated the systems. In the background he could hear the storage compartments open and close. Together they used the cargo restraints to secure the extra equipment from the repairs, along with the damaged parts he had replaced.

After a hasty meal of nutrition bars and water, he let her have the first turn in the freshener. When he emerged after his turn, she was standing in the doorway. Coming up behind her, he looked out at the purple plains, where the sun was reaching the mountains. "Blue?"

She touched the controls and sealed the door. "Gone."

He wanted to give her another hug, but there was no time. If aught went amiss he did not wish to attempt an emergency landing in the dark. "Fasten in."

Dropping into the pilot's chair he fastened his restraints with one hand, powering up the console with the other. "You did give her a tracker."

Her sigh was heartbreaking. "I did, but it is better for Blue if I do not look for her when we return."

Turning his attention to the controls, he initiated communications. "Hyssop to *Nightingale*. We are coming home."

***

For the first half-period of transit, the DOP-C was silent. Bran needed to keep his focus on safely exiting the atmosphere. Once in the expanse, a propulsion failure would be inconvenient, but they had sufficient fuel and air to survive until the *Nightingale* could collect them.

The sky deepened to dark navy, and clouds hid the plains. The engines hummed, pushing against the outer atmosphere. Stars shimmered into view, and the last of the blue turned to black as they entered the beaconless expanse. He checked the trajectory and made a minute adjustment. The *Nightingale* was east and a few degrees north, at the edge of the planet's shadow.

It was safe to shift his attention to Adriana, but words would not come. He knew it would not end well when she named the terrier. She was not even aware of him, her gaze a thousand miles away, or a thousand inward.

"Another period," he said. He cringed as he spoke, but it was better than the heavy silence. "It will be seventh bell after midday on the *Nightingale*." The banalities leapt from his mouth, one after the other. Adriana knew that the *Nightingale* maintained orbit at the midpoint of the area under survey.

Her chin lifted, dark eyes meeting his as she returned from wherever she had been. "It is well. I want to secure the samples in my office, and it will be easier to do with no one in the lab."

"Do you fear tampering?"

Her lips twisted. "I fear that the DOP-C might not be the only victim of the saboteur. I do not want these samples turning to goop."

"How hard is that to do? Sabotage your analysis instruments?"

"It does not require sabotage as such. Simply someone with the appropriate access to reset the configuration and expose the samples to excess scan energy. The trick would be in altering the logs to hide the deliberate recalibration."

The hair on the back of his neck rose. Whoever was causing their problems had a high degree of systems knowledge to sabotage both the DOP-C and laboratory instruments. "Who do you know with the skills?"

"Any of the zoologists or botanists could turn the sample to goop. But hide their access to the systems afterward?" She shook her head. "I have the command codes for it, and Leonardo's Botany lead. Other than that"—she held out her hands in a helpless gesture—"nobody I know of on either team has the skills to circumvent the controls."

"I doubt the botanist could sabotage a DOP-C, but I will look at him."

She nodded. "From his dossier, I cannot imagine when he would have had the time to acquire engineering skills."

He could not quite believe she voiced that. "Are we admitting to our respective cartels' profiling?"

She chuckled without mirth. "It was a ridiculous pretense from the start. Now? I doubt Serengeti has aught that is not known to Matahorn, but if you are willing to share, I will speak with Security Chief Lochan. He is surprisingly reasonable for one dedicated to paranoia and stealth."

The Matahorn security chief was why Bran, and not Caoimh—the third Phoenix Enterprises partner—was on this voyage. After the disaster of Jarrod-Sadico, Monsignor Horatio would only tolerate a Serengeti captain if Matahorn controlled security. Raleigh would not voyage into the unknown without one of his two trusted partners at his back.

Raleigh wanted Bran for navigator, but Monsignor Hercules of Grey Spear and Serengeti controlled that role and would not yield it. Grey Spear's function within Serengeti was logistics and supply, but at its core was a vast database of navigational routes. Data they did not share.

None of which would be secret from Adriana with her access to the dossiers built by Matahorn. That did not change Bran's situation. "Lochan is not above suspicion. As of this moment, only you and Nickolas are above it."

Her chuckle turned to a glower. She opened her mouth and yipped.

Yipped? That sound had come from the cargo area. It could not be, but it was. Blue, perched on a crate, wagged her tail in greeting.

***

Adriana stared at Blue. The little dog should not be on the DOP-C, but Adriana's heart did not care.

Bran's hard voice broke her trance. "Adriana. What did you do?"

His expression was as stern as his voice. It wounded her even as she recognized he could not be blamed for his suspicion. "On my honor, I did not bring her on board."

His eyebrows rose. "How, then?"

"No notion." She looked back at the dog. "Where would I have put her? The storage areas are packed. We did the cargo together."

His expression softened by degrees. "I beg your pardon. But how can she be here?"

Adriana turned back to the dog. "Blue, what is your secret? How did you get past us? Where did you hide?"

With a doggy grin, Blue bounded off the crate, touched the floor and sprang into Adriana's lap.

She ran her hands over the terrier, finding no sign of injury. "Her fur is surprisingly soft under the rough outer coat. And slick."

Bran huffed. "Not useful."

He was right. Adriana continued to stroke Blue, her thoughts seeking an explanation. With a contented sound, Blue snuggled down and curled into a ball. She was a bit large for Adriana's lap, but not heavy. Adriana adjusted her position and cradled the dog comfortably. "It had to be after we finished with the cargo. She is incredibly fast. Were you at the console when I was in the freshener?"

"I was." His eyes narrowed. "You cannot think she streaked past me unnoticed. Nothing is that fast."

"She was a blur going after that snake." Adriana looked over at the cargo. "If she tucked in behind the crates, she would be easy to miss."

"I am not so unobservant I would have missed her when I left the freshener."

"Are you certain? We were within minutes of launch. Your mind would have been on that."

His eyes narrowed, his gaze dropping to her lap. "Where is the animal?"

"Asleep in my lap?" Amused, she looked down at her hand, resting on her lap. A lap apparently empty of the dog she could feel. "She is here. I can feel her."

Adriana's fingers tightened in the fur, the tips disappearing into the gray of her uniform . . . or not her uniform. "Blue?"

Two glowing blue eyes appeared amidst the gray. A ring of white surrounded them and spread outward until Blue was once again a little white dog.

Bran's voice was a whisper. "Five Warriors and Adelaide. What is she?"

Adriana could feel her cheeks stretch with a grin. "Blue is incontrovertible evidence that the ancients had a hand in the Thirteenth System." She scratched the creature's ears. "For her to change color, specialized nanocrystals would have to be introduced to her hair follicles. They are found in some species of lizards, but not in mammals."

Bran's eyes narrowed. "A dog-lizard hybrid?"

She considered the implications. "Cross-species hybridization is theoretically possible, but we do not have the technologistics."

The little creature in her lap closed its eyes and relaxed under Adriana's absent stroking.

"How does it do it? Is it intentional?"

It was a sound query, but all Adriana could offer was speculation. "I think when she fell asleep it was a survival mechanism. When she hunts, it could be instinct or intent. I would need to run tests."

Bran blinked his eyes. "You said she was white when she took out that snake."

"Then, but before that, I did not see her. Yesterday morning, I saw the plants move against the breeze, but not Blue until she was clear of the plants. She seemed to appear out of nowhere this morning."

Bran's voice low, he nodded at her lap. "It is doing it now."

Adriana's eyes dropped but her fingers never altered their rhythm. Gray matching the uniform formed splotches that grew until there was no sign of white.

Bran shook his head. "Now that I am watching, I can make out its outline, extra mass between your lap and your waist. Incredible."

She shared his wonder, but it was tempered with fear. "We will need to get her back to the surface as soon as possible. Do you think Captain Raleigh would consider giving me a DOP-C for a camp? We need to study Blue, and we dare not keep her on the *Nightingale*."

The DOP-Cs were critical resources for exploration, but evidence of ancients' genetic manipulation skills was priceless. The console chimed, taking Bran's attention.

"You can ask the captain yourself. He and Nickolas are going to meet us in the launch bay."

"Does the captain know about Blue?"

"No. And I do not think it wise to mention her on an open communications channel."

She nodded at his caution. "Someone was willing to turn genetic samples to goop." She glanced at her lap. "I will keep her with me until I can return her to Deuce."

***

The final half period of the flight was as quiet as its start. Adriana had returned to her thousand-mile stare, and Bran did not blame her. She had voiced Blue was impossible, and she could not have been more accurate. For unknown reasons, the ancients had bred a chameleon terrier. A domesticated breed that had somehow survived abandonment when the ancients disappeared at the beginning of the Anarchy.

When the *Nightingale* came into visual contact, Bran shut away his wonderment and focused on maneuvering the DOP-C through the increasing gravity and into its slot. As hoped, the bay was vacant but for the duty sergeant and a mechanic. If the Leonardo militia sergeant wondered at Bran's refusal to allow maintenance access to the DOP-C, he was too well-trained to voice it.

As soon as Adriana released her restraints, Blue turned white. Adriana looked at Bran. "We could improvise a leash, but I doubt she would tolerate it. If I tuck her inside my jacket, can you make a sling from one of the cargo ties?"

Why did he find her resourcefulness so endearing? "Give me a moment, but we are going to need something more secure than a sling."

Blue was surprisingly docile as Bran created an X-shaped harness. Adriana softened under his touch as he bound the tie across her shoulders and around her waist. Was it his hands on her that caused her blush? The bondage that had her swaying toward him? Breathing deeply of the spicy scent that clung to her from the planet, he forced himself to step back. When the time came to explore what was happening between them, he would remember her response.

A deep bass voice rumbled from the doorway. "Should I return later?"

Captain Raleigh leaned against the doorframe, his arms crossed, a half smile on his face. Dark-skinned with close-cropped black hair and black eyes above prominent cheekbones, he topped Bran by four inches and had a breadth of shoulder to match. Physically sparring with the captain was challenging. Mentally sparring even more so.

Bran stepped away, embarrassed to be so caught up in Adriana he did not notice Raleigh's approach. "It is not what it appears." He moved aside. "The Lt. Commander has a passenger."

One pointed ear, two glowing blue eyes, and a narrow snout emerged from the opening in Adriana's jacket.

Raleigh's amused expression shifted to ire. "Have you lost your wits? You know what occurred the last time you brought live subjects to the *Nightingale*."

"It is not what you think," Adriana said. "We did not bring her. She stowed away."

Raleigh barked a mirthless laugh. "Bran?"

"It is complicated." He moved to the area where Adriana's samples were stored. "The short version is that Blue is an ancients' artifact."

***

Bran watched Raleigh and Nickolas go from disbelief to bewilderment to fascination while Adriana explained about finding Blue. Or Blue finding Adriana. Her private office was the securest chamber in the lab section, and she refused to store her precious samples anywhere else. Before she began her explanations, Bran secured the monitors. It was not impossible for Lochan to bypass Raleigh's and Bran's commands, but they would know if he tried.

Adriana perched on the desk, giving the desk chair to Raleigh, the guest chair to Bran, and leaving Nickolas propped against a wall. Blue, released from restraint, explored every centimeter.

Stretching out his legs, Raleigh crossed his ankles. "I can justify a DOP-C to study Blue and her environment for a day. Two at the most. Even then, it will be at least a day to prepare. Unless you plan to take your artifact back to the surface in the next bell, it will not remain hidden."

Adriana rolled her shoulders, expression tight with strain. "I plan to keep her with me. I do not think anyone will try to take her by force. Where would they go?"

Raleigh chuckled. "Keeping her with you could get messy."

"Nothing I have not dealt with before."

Bran stifled a yawn. He could see his weariness reflected in Adriana. They were both overtired and stressed from the crash and its aftermath.

She glanced at the terrier who was using a back paw to scratch one ear. "And she should be safe from the plague for a day. It was sevenday before it affected the other samples."

As if knowing she had Adriana's attention, Blue settled at her feet, eyes hopeful. Adriana sighed. "I can give you water. But I have no notion what to feed you."

"What about part of the snake-thing?" Nickolas asked. "She killed it. She might eat it."

Adriana blinked and then nodded. "I need to take some scans, but that will not take long. After that, I do not need the entire carcass."

Raleigh pushed out of the chair. "It nears ninth bell. Unless you think she will starve before morning, I would have you and Bran get a meal and some rest."

Bran's stomach rumbled. "Adriana?"

"Blue will be fine." Leaving the desk, she rooted around in a cabinet, emerging with a small sample container and some absorbent pads. "This will work for water, and the pads will provide a decent bed.

Crouching by Blue, Nickolas scratched her chin, his deep chuckle filling the chamber. "I wish I could be there where Katleen learns of this."

Raleigh's eyebrows rose. "Is she not enamored of that tree wombat?"

Nickolas' chuckle turned to laughter. "It only sparkles. This one, changes hue."

At Adriana's bewildered expression, Bran explained. "Katleen is Lilian Thornraven's young sister. She made a pet of an abandoned wombat pup."

Adriana's expression flattened. "Blue and I will be in my cabin."

Confused by her sudden coldness, Bran stepped in Adriana's path. "What is amiss?"

"Naught. Message received."

"What message?"

Her soft snort held as much pain as derision. "This is a Serengeti vessel and venture. Lieutenant Nickolas is close commerce-kin to Monsignor Lucius and his consort Lilian Thornraven, while I was given a place to placate an important investor. "

Nickolas surged to his feet. "That is ludicrous. Your skills are unquestioned. As for the rest . . ." He motioned with one hand. "Monsignor Lucius was as careful in his placements as Monsignor Horatio. Neither will risk the success of this venture."

"As Lt. Clarence is so quick to point out."

Bran was more confused. "Clarence? Your second?"

"My *Serengeti warrior* second. And only second so Serengeti could control the command crew."

Nickolas' eyes narrowed and his friendly tones turned silky. "Clarence voiced that?"

Crossing her arms over her middle, she met his gaze with a defiant tilt of her chin. "Often."

"Demon scat." Raleigh's glower matched Bran's reaction. "I thought the crew more cohesive."

Nickolas shook his head. "The flyer pilots are unified. But we had extensive training as a group." He considered a moment. "I have not noticed such divisions in the maintenance engineers."

Raleigh rubbed his chin. "The command crew is sensitive to security-privilege, but otherwise work well together."

If possible, Adriana's chin tipped higher. "So, it is only my leadership that is lacking?"

"What say you?" Bran grasped her shoulders. "No one holds any such belief. If Lt. Clarence is a lone malcontent, he is readily dealt with before he can spread his poison. The question is whether those attitudes affect other areas. We have enough trouble from the saboteur. We do not need divisiveness undermining morale."

Adriana's shoulders softened in his hands. Her chin lowered. "I beg your pardon. I am overtired, and the lieutenant has been more aggravating than usual."

"How so?"

A blush tinted her cheeks, her eyes going to Raleigh and Nickolas watching in bemusement. She shrugged and Bran released her. "Adriana?"

"His work is lackluster at best. I cannot determine if it is lack of skill or laziness." She looked past Bran to Raleigh. "I have documented his lack of productivity. I expected a replacement when we returned to Fortuna for repairs. That he remained gives credence to his claims."

Consternation replaced Raleigh's bemusement. "We were focused on replacing those lost in battle. Unless a crew member had a disciplinary action or ties to known despoilers, we did not make changes. There was no time."

Blue crowded Adriana's ankles, making a soft sound. Her expression easing, she lifted the creature into her arms. "I suppose the result is worth it. If I could trust Lt. Clarence's work, he would have gone to Deuce to the collect the samples."

"His work is that that bad?"

"Bad enough." She looked at Bran. "It gives further weight to his claims. That one so unworthy is on the *Nightingale* can only be due to Blooded Dagger patronage."

Nickolas snorted. "Monsignor is devoted to his cartouche, but he does not offer patronage to the unworthy. He has exiled *seigneurs* for failing to meet his standards of honor and commerce."

Adriana's eyes widened. Exiling a signet-bearing warrior was no minor matter. "I have no response to that, Lt. Nickolas, but Lt. Clarence's behavior is as I have voiced."

Before Nickolas could respond, Raleigh held up a hand. "I do not doubt you. But we will not resolve this tonight. Let us reconvene at the tenth bell. If it is limited to Lt. Clarence, it is an annoyance. If his attitudes are more widespread, we will need to act."

5. Genetic Memory

Sevenday 32, Day 1

    Adriana opened her eyes to the sound of energetic lapping. Rolling toward the sound, she found Blue at the makeshift water dish. Last night, the little creature had ignored the pallet of absorbent pads, leaping onto the bed with Adriana. Although she knew it was unwise, Adriana allowed her to remain. It was better than missing Bran's strong arms around her. She had almost invited him in when he escorted her to her door, but after the discussion about Clarence, she was feeling a bit raw as well as embarrassed. There was no question she was overtired, and her emotions were unstable. Her cabin has seemed like a refuge for about a half period. By the time her emotions settled, it was too late.

    Stretching in the bed highlighted residual soreness from the crash, and probably various other strains brought on by their activities afterward. A much-needed shower before bed had revealed a range of bruises. A glance out her small window showed the bright glow of the system's sun, muted by shading. While she had slept, the *Nightingale*'s orbit moved it between the planet and its star.

    Swinging her legs over the side of the bed, she started to reach for her slate to contact Bran. For what purpose? A good-morning greeting? She dragged her scattered thoughts to order. There would be time to explore her developing relationship with Bran. First, she needed to process those samples, beginning with that snake. Judging from the rate Blue emptied the water dish, the little thing was hungry. So was Adriana. The small, reconstituted vegetable roll she liberated from the galley was long gone.

As if hearing her thoughts, Blue bounced over, blue eyes glowing. "Yes, I am planning to feed you."

Blue rose on her haunches and placed her front paws in Adriana's lap. Amused, she rubbed the terrier's ears. "Good morning to you, too."

With a gentle nudge, she set the dog on the floor and rose from the bed. "I will need a few minutes and then we are off to the lab to see about that snake."

In less than a quarter period she was freshened, dressed, and ready for the day. Leaving the freshener, she found Blue had used the absorbent pads for her own morning activities. "Well done, Blue. Your spoor will reveal much about your diet and health."

Before leaving the cabin, Adriana alerted Bran she was heading to the lab. It was appropriate communication, and if he wished to meet her there, he would. Shouldering her slate satchel and the sample case with Blue's output, she gathered up the terrier. Unlike when they arrived, the corridors were not empty, and more than one crew member gave Blue a curious glance. Although most of the crew had little interaction with the zoology team, all had been fascinated by the creatures brought back for study. More than one had sorrowed over their untimely deaths.

***

Bran was waiting when she arrived at her office. His smile of welcome lifted her heart, and she felt her cheeks stretch with an answering smile.

He reached for the sample case. "What is this?"

"Blue's spoor. She made the deposit on the pad."

"That was fortunate."

Securing the door, she set down Blue. "The deposit was dead center."

His eyebrows rose. "Are you certain it was not luck? The pad happened to be where she squatted?"

"My cabin is not that small. She had to seek out the pad." Leaving Blue to explore, Adriana opened her vault and pulled out the snake sample. "Join me in the lab?"

"Of course." He held out his hand. "I will carry the samples so you can carry Blue."

"She should follow me as she did on Deuce. I carried her from my quarters to protect her. As it was, three crew members asked to pet her."

"Is that bad?"

"Probably not. The gloves we use to handle the creatures on Deuce are designed to protect us, not them, but they are all well. Even the ones set with trackers a month ago. But, until I know what killed the specimens we brought on board, the fewer who handle Blue, the better. I should not have let Nickolas pet her, but I was tired and not thinking clearly."

Stepping aside, he let her lead the way into the lab area. "How long will you need with the snake?"

"Half a period. In addition to scans, I want a sample of its venom. Tissue and other samples can wait."

"It is about time you arrived." Lt. Clarence was at the central console with the Leonardo and Matahorn team members. "We have been waiting nearly a period for the new samples."

It was not yet half past the eighth bell. At worst she was a half period later than her norm. Annoyed at feeling defensive, she ignored the lieutenant and moved to the scanner. "You will have a bit longer to wait. I have one sample for immediate processing, and I will tend to it. Meanwhile, have you started on mapping the trackers I placed during the mission?"

"I assigned that to Tricia. Hardly worth my time."

The Leonardo scientist was their entomologist and could not be spared to handle Clarence's tasks. "I assigned the work to you. Tricia has sufficient tasks of her own."

"Do not forget that I am Serengeti. I have every right to review the samples and no time to waste on minor tasks."

Bran's voice cut in. "Lt. Clarence, you are insubordinate."

Clarence whipped around to face the doorway where Bran stood. "Commander. I did not see you. How can I assist?"

"By following Lt. Commander Adriana's orders."

A low growl came from the area near Adriana's ankles. The hair on Blue's back was up and her gaze was focused on Clarence.

The zoologist whipped back around, his eyes widening. "Socraide's sword." He lifted his gaze to Adriana. "You brought a feral canine on board and have not caged it?"

"Blue is not feral. She simply does not like you."

Bran snorted while Tricia made a suspicious-sounding cough. Govind, the Matahorn zoologist, bit his lip, his eyes dancing.

Clarence sputtered, his eyes narrowing. "This is not a jesting matter. Of course it is feral."

"Do not contradict the lieutenant commander," Bran said. "I have spent three days with the creature, and Blue is better behaved than you."

"We do not have time for this." Adriana pulled out the snake. "I need to process this sample and then the captain requires my presence." Using the shocked silence at the sight of the snake, she continued, "A full briefing will be provided when the captain approves it. Until then, accept that the little canine is not feral and is not to be touched."

Placing the sample by the scanner, she motioned to Govind. "You will assist me. Tricia, please return to the tasks *I* assigned. Clarence, you are responsible for mapping the trackers."

Clarence prepared to protest, but a glance at Bran silenced him. With a curt nod, he moved to his station.

Flashing Adriana a smile, Bran claimed a chair at the console and pulled out his slate. "Have you had a morning meal? No? I will have something brought from the galley and wait until you and Blue are ready to join Raleigh."

Flushing with pleasure at his care for her, Adriana turned to the console.

***

Adriana smiled at Nickolas as she put the container of chopped snake in front of Blue. "It was an excellent suggestion. From her spoor sample, it is consistent with her diet."

Nickolas chuckled as Blue attacked her meal. "Pleased to assist."

Raleigh cleared his throat. "Did you discover anything else of interest?"

"Genetically, it is a snake, although not an exact match to any known species. Its venom is a neurotoxin, but readily countered now that we have it analyzed. Although, multiple bites could be deadly."

"What are the chances of multiple bites?"

"Low. It takes some time for the sac to refill." She considered a moment. "If someone fell into a nest with multiple snakes, that could be a problem."

Raleigh's lips twitched. "Bran, make a note. Planet teams are to avoid snake nests."

She started to take offense at his levity and then realized he was teasing her. With as much primness as she could muster, Adriana said, "Free-traders have an odd sense of humor."

Raleigh burst out laughing and was soon joined by Bran and Nickolas. "And I should remember that scientists are known to be quick witted."

The captain asked, "What of Blue? Bran tells us she used the pad in your cabin as if properly trained. Which we know is impossible."

"About that." Adriana glanced at Blue who was gulping the chopped snake. "I have a theory. It would explain her comfort with us and other behavior."

Raleigh leaned in. "Which is?"

Scientifically, her answer was far-fetched, but it fit the facts. "Genetic memory."

"Genetic memory?" Raleigh cocked his head. "Is that where birds instinctively know to migrate?"

"Perhaps," she said. "The hypothesis that animals pass knowledge from one generation to another through genetically stored memory has been around for centuries. Avian migration is at the core of what research exists, but it does not quite meet the test of empirical evidence. For truth, there is not much commerce value in the proposition, so research is spotty."

"Then why do you think that genetic memory accounts for Blue's behavior?"

"Because the alternative is that she is over a millennium old, which I have already eliminated." She glanced at Blue who was licking the bowl. "Unless you think there is a hidden group of sentients on this planet that raised her, genetic memory is the only other option."

Nickolas grinned. "When the impossible is eliminated, whatever is left, no matter how improbable, must be the truth."

Both Bran and Raleigh chuckled at the quote from a popular free-trader entertainment. One that even Adriana had used to fill the bells on their long voyage. "Given that the ancients were able to craft a canine with chameleon attributes, not even that improbable. And quite practical if they wished to transport their companions through the stellar expanse. I would not relish attempting to train a new puppy while in stellar transit."

The little canine chose that moment to launch herself into Adriana's lap.

With a bemused expression, Bran ran his fingers through his hair, pushing the shaggy mane off his forehead. "Could they have gone further? For a dog you met two days ago, she appears to have bonded as if it were two months. Have you any notion of Blue's age?"

"How far did the ancients go with their genetic tinkering?" Adriana gave Blue's ears a gentle tug. "I will need to run more analysis. Assuming Blue's lifespan is similar to other domestic canines her size, somewhere between two and three years."

"Assuming?"

"The lizard genetic material could have shortened her life span," She looked down into bright blue eyes hoping that was not the case.

"But then, given all the other genetic manipulation, the ancients could have elongated it. It will take time to run the tests, and until my team has met the current mission parameters, determining Blue's life expectancy is not a priority." She tried to keep the hope out of her voice as she turned to the Raleigh, "Unless the captain has a different view?"

He shook his head. "I am as curious as any, but unless you can do it during the two days' grace you have for studying her environment, completing the mapping and surveys must come first."

***

Perched on a mechanic's stool, Bran waited while Raleigh examined the damaged propulsion module. The maintenance bay had been sealed since Bran's return. Neither he nor the captain were willing to risk the saboteur destroying evidence. Nor was it wise to have Bran as the only witness to the sabotage. As captain, Raleigh had ultimate authority and accountability. When they located the perpetrator, one or more powerful warriors were likely to challenge the indictment.

Straightening, Raleigh's expression was grim. "Your zoologist knows that the propulsion unit was sabotaged, but not the rest?"

It was on the tip of Bran's tongue to correct Raleigh that Adriana was not *his*. But that was what Bran wanted and he was not reluctant to stake a claim. "She is clever enough to have questioned more, but she was out setting her lures when I did most of the repairs. She knows that navigation was damaged, but I let her believe it happened during the crash."

Raleigh turned his attention to the navigational unit. "It could be that they simply damaged critical systems in the hope one would fail."

Bran waited. The captain knew the systems as well as he.

Raleigh traced through the damaged components. "They managed to leave everything operational for launch, but weakened to the point where the stress of planet entry would do the rest." He closed the unit and perched on the console. "Best case for the saboteur, navigation would fail, and you would have been far off course before the crash. We might have spent sevendays searching."

With a grim sigh, Bran nodded. "I suspect they made certain of the propulsion. Navigation was a bonus if it resulted in the *Nightingale* spending sevendays searching."

"The bigger question is, what was their goal?"

Bran had long periods on the planet to consider the matter. "The three DOP-Cs retained by the *Nightingale* after our ospreys returned to the Eleventh System are essential to making up the time lost in the battle and its aftermath. Destroying one would hinder us, as would the loss of a pilot and a scientist. But could they be certain who would be the next to use that DOP-C?"

"If it is true that the destruction of the zoology samples was sabotage, then Adriana was the target. What did you make of Clarence?"

"She understated the matter. The man was blatantly insubordinate and in front of the rest of the team. It is possible he destroyed the samples out of spite, but sabotage?" Bran shrugged. "Too obvious. Adversarial agents do not call attention to themselves."

"Check him out anyway." Raleigh pushed off the console. "And Bran, if we cannot lay this on Clarence, we will need to inform Trevelyan."

Lucius Mercio's spymaster was one of the few seigneurs Bran and Raleigh trusted not to be biased by the status and familial alliances among the crew. Communications between the Thirteenth System and Serengeti Headquarters were difficult. Short, coded messages could take half a day. Full reports two or three days. It was cumbersome, and they had hoped the saboteur would be discovered before they needed to notify Serengeti Headquarters. Now that the saboteur's actions had escalated to life-threatening, Bran knew they had no choice.

Raleigh continued, "At the very least, Trevelyan's operatives have the resources to evaluate the crew for those with skills to sabotage Adriana's experiments and tamper with the DOP-C."

"Other than the two of us and Lochan."

"Lochan came to me with suspicions about a saboteur after your DOP-C crashed."

Bran sat back. "It could be sincere, or a ploy to throw us off."

"As you voiced. I ordered him to investigate and report his findings." Raleigh rubbed his jaw. "I wish I could rule him out, but we dare not let ourselves be biased."

***

Four bells later, Bran found Adriana where he expected, in the zoology lab, focused on an instrument console. Her expression intent, she was oblivious to his arrival. He knew Blue would be close, but it took him a moment to locate her. She was curled up by Adriana's feet, perfectly blended into the beige polymer tile.

In the segmented lab chambers, Tricia and Govind were focused on their tasks. There was no sign of Clarence. His review confirmed all Adriana had said the night before. Had matters not been so dire after the battle, Lt. Clarence would have been discharged. The man was useless. To Bran's regret, he lacked the skills to be the saboteur and had alibis for at least two incidents. It had been an unlikely chance. On the bright side, Bran could intimidate the scum-sucking rodent without endangering the *Nightingale*.

Skirting the console so he could approach through Adriana's line of sight, he said her name.

Her head came up and she blinked. "Bran." She blinked again and stretched. "What bell? How long—? Oh, it nears fifth bell. I beg your pardon. I lost track. I need a period to prepare for the planet."

"We can leave now, but it will be dark when we land. If Blue is safe for another night, I would wait until tomorrow."

Adriana's gaze dropped to the now white canine who was looking up at her with bright interest. Lifting her gaze back to Bran, she started to speak and then stopped. Her eyes went to Tricia and

Govind, neither of whom looked up.

Half covering her mouth, Adriana said, "Blue may be in danger. I do not believe the risk is with the *Nightingale*, but one of her crew. I need another two periods to finish this analysis and then I will know more."

"I will schedule our launch for tomorrow, ninth bell before midday." He looked around the almost silent lab. Neither of the other zoologists seemed a threat, but years of fighting pirates taught him not to trust appearances. "I will bring an evening meal and wait with you."

The relief in her eyes confirmed his instincts. Whatever she thought she had discovered, it was dangerous. Turning her head, she half covered her mouth again. "If they have planet-foraged meat, ask for some that is raw."

He started to ask and noticed he had Tricia and Govind's attention. "Whatever you need."

***

It took Bran less than a period to return with their meals and what he assumed was Blue's. Tricia had left but Govind was still bent over his instruments. At Adriana's direction, Bran set the tray on a small table that seemed to exist for that purpose.

Her voice bright, Adriana exclaimed over the fare, "Deuce elk, how marvelous."

The four-footed grazers were smaller than Twelve Systems elk, and closer in taste to venison. Bran knew that the zoologists had a scientific name for the beasts, but they used a colloquial term to make the food more familiar to the crew. When possible, the galley supplemented their preserved and hydroponic rations with local foraging. It was always popular and went fast.

As Bran was certain Adriana intended, Govind shut down his instruments and rose. "Adriana, do you need anything else?"

With a casual wave, she shook her head. "Enjoy your evening."

As the door recessed behind the man, Bran started to ask the questions teeming at the tip of his tongue. Adriana held up a hand and then slowly folded her fingers, one at a time. When she had a fist, she rose and went to the entrance. Her fingers danced on the control panel and amber lights signaled they were sealed in.

Her expression determined, she said, "I have sealed the monitors to my authority."

Bran, Raleigh, and Lochan could override that seal, but no others. "What have you discovered?"

"At the moment, it is a well-founded suspicion. Another half period and I will have certainty." She reached the table where Blue was eagerly sniffing. "Not long now, Blue."

She lifted dish covers until she found the raw portion. Cutting a small piece, she placed it in a sample dish and then the analysis unit.

The technology had many uses, and one was common in the medical enclaves. "Do you seek drugs or poison?"

"They are often the same thing," she replied. "This is a bit more complicated. I am using a bit of the snake for comparison."

"What do you expect to find?"

"Nothing in the Deuce elk that should not be there."

"Why are you being so evasive?"

Her eyes widened, and chagrin spread across her features. "I beg your pardon. In science, we are not specific until there is certainty. More than one zoologist has had a career collapse for speaking too soon. Someone is always seeking to make a reputation by bringing down another."

"I did not realize scientists were so ruthless."

"You have no idea." She sat next to him, her eyes on the analysis unit. "After our meeting with the captain, I was thinking about snake venom and the different types. If one did not know it was caused by a snake bite, some hemotoxins can appear as a blood-borne disease. Certain plants are also hemotoxins. The symptoms displayed by our dead samples fit a hemotoxin."

"You did not check for poison on samples that died?"

"Of course we did. And found nothing. That is why we postulated that something benign to us was toxic to the samples. But if it were an unknown toxin, like that snake's was until today"—she shrugged—"It would not be difficult for a zoologist or botanist to smuggle an unknown toxin on board."

The unit chimed and Adriana checked the results, a relieved smile forming. "Good news, Blue, Deuce elk for dinner."

Not bothering to cut the meat, she set the plate on the floor. Snatching her meal, Blue carried it off to a corner where she gripped it between two paws. Sharp teeth tore off a good-sized chunk. Bran whistled. "For such a sweet-looking creature, that is an impressive set of teeth."

"Powerful jaw, too." Adriana wiped her hands on a cleaning cloth. "She killed that snake by severing its brain stem."

Bran lifted the covers, pushing a plate closer to Adriana. "Why not feed Blue more snake?"

"It has been poisoned."

"What say you?"

"When I butchered the snake for Blue's breakfast, I used a section we did not need for analysis. There was enough for a second meal." She looked over at Blue. The dog had reduced its meal by two thirds. "If I had not been thinking about poisoning, I might not have noticed that the meat had been handled. Whoever did it, poisoned the sample as well."

"How do you know it is poisoned?"

"There were chemicals present that had not been there before."

"Could they have been overlooked?"

"A good, skeptical, scientific question. But I had the results of the analysis I ran while classifying the venom. It did not show a trace of the chemical. Since then, I isolated the chemical for analysis. In another"—she glanced at the time—"ten minutes, we will know what it does, and if I am right."

Bran's stomach growled, reminding him he bypassed the midday meal. "Watching the time will not make it pass. And the elk is getting cold."

Adriana may have skipped her midday meal as well, because after a tentative first bite, she made quick work of the meat. She had speared a vegetable when the unit chimed. Abandoning her plate, she rushed to the console. There was tension in every line of her back as she accessed the results.

When she turned, her expression was a fierce blend of grim determination and triumph. "Plant-based hemotoxin of unknown origin."

A shiver ran down his spine. The words popped out before the thought was formed. "You and Blue should stay with me tonight."

Adriana's eyes widened, and her expression turned quizzical.

"For your protection," he blurted out and watched her eyebrows rise. "And my peace of mind."

Her lips curved in a soft smile. "I am torn between surprise at what I thought was a rather graceless proposition, and being flattered that you would worry about us to such a degree."

"Us? Right. I think you could protect Blue. I am less certain she could do aught against a fireburst pistol. Or a well-handled dagger."

Adriana's expression sobered. "For truth, I suspect I would not slumber with ease knowing that someone is intent on Blue's death. We accept your invitation."

***

Cradling Blue, Adriana followed Bran through his quarters. She was not surprised that the first officer's quarters were twice the size of hers. In addition to a bedchamber with a sizable bed, there was a small sitting area. The private freshener was standard with no more than a step between fixtures. She had not expected the small personal touches, assuming Bran's quarters would be as austere as the man. The silky throw was a random pattern of blues and greens. A small oil painting of a cottage by a lake could have been from Socraide Prime if it were not for the hint of violet in the water and the deep blue sky.

Looking up from the painting, she asked, "Your home? The

Eleventh System?"

"Twelfth." Sorrow touched his eyes. "It was my wife's childhood home. I have not been there in a while, but the painting brings serenity."

His pirate-murdered wife. "I am sorry for your loss."

He took her satchel and set it on the bed. "It was a long time ago."

It was clear that he did not wish to discuss his deceased spouse. Suddenly feeling awkward and uncertain, she suggested, "I can sleep on the little sofa."

"Do not be ridiculous." He straightened with a jerk. "The bed is big enough for us both. And it is not as if it will be the first time."

She could feel heat suffusing her cheeks at the memory of being curled against his chest. "Yes. Well. That is . . . we are intruding."

His eyes darkened with confusion. "What troubles you?"

Before she could control her reaction, her eyes went to the painting. She snapped them back to meet his gaze, but it was too late. His jaw hardened, his lips a stern line.

"I am sorry." Embarrassed, she backed up. "It is not a topic . . . I did not mean to intrude. It was an innocent question." She slammed her lips together to halt her babbling. It was Evander all over again. Apologizing without knowing how she had erred.

Tears pricked, and her throat burned. Turning, she fled through the door into the smaller chamber. Part of her wanted to keep running and return to her quarters, but her tactlessness was not a valid reason to endanger Blue. Unless Bran asked her to leave, she would stay.

Setting Blue down, she rifled through her satchel for the pads and water dish. The sofa proved comfortable and would be fine for a night. Ignoring the pads, Blue bounced onto the sofa to curl against Adriana. Adoring blue eyes assured her that, at least in Blue's opinion, Adriana was wonderful. Fondling the dog's ears, she shook her head. "After Evander, you would think I would know better than to weave fantasies of romance from a few kisses."

"It offends me to be compared to that conniving wastrel"—Bran spoke from the doorway—"but I fear I have earned it with my taciturn behavior."

His remorseful expression matching his tone, he moved into the chamber. "Please forgive me."

"I was not prying."

"I know." He gestured to the sofa. "May I?"

He was asking permission to sit on *his* sofa. It was somehow both ludicrous and reassuring. At Adriana's nod, he settled next to her.

He clasped his hands between his knees, his gaze on the floor. "I do not often speak of Odette. But perhaps not for the reasons you might expect. When I *think* of her, it is with remembered joy. Too often, *speaking* of her unlocks an unabating rage that Matahorn left us at the mercy of the pirates while exacting a usurious tribute. Anger that the rest of the Twelve Systems left us to fight the pirates alone for more than a year."

She wished she could deny his charges, but she could not. No wonder he became so taciturn "I had no notion. It was all so distant and seemed unrelated to my life." Her heart aching, she reached for his hand. "I beg your pardon. I had no notion."

He squeezed her fingers. "Peace. Other than Lucius Mercio, few in the primary three systems understood. Or cared. I have not the whole of it, but we know Mercio used ruthless means to gain the governing council's support to take a fleet against Sadico."

She was of the First System and as guilty of indifference as any other."I was thirty-two and wooed by a Margovian Warrior. I accepted the media assertions that the piracy was free-trader thugs fighting for territory. Even then, I knew something was amiss. My parents educated me on the corruption in the media feeds, but I was self-absorbed. I convinced myself that if aught were seriously awry the governing council would act."

"The governing council is no more honorable than any other set of warriors. And Matahorn controls the council."

Adriana's heart ached at Bran's words. There was truth to his claim and justification for his hostility toward Matahorn. But a great deal had changed in the last decade. She feared if she could not break through his distrust for all things Matahorn, they had no future. She turned her head to meet his gaze. "Our preeminence is not as bad as you believe. I have reason to know that Monsignor Horatio joined the armada to rescue the Thirteenth System out of shame, not bravado."

Bran stiffened, his expression turning dark.

She would not shrink from this. "Before my consort alliance dissolved, my youngest sister formed a friendship with Mistress Lorelie."

"Horatio's youngest?"

Monsignor Horatio claimed six offspring: his heir, William, from a consort alliance, and five more from his warrior spouse. "Seigneur William's favorite sibling."

"Explain."

"My knowledge is secondhand, but my sister is no dupe. Monsignor Horatio regretted resisting Monsignor Lucius' petition for aid against the pirates all those years ago. At the time, he thought it was a Serengeti plot to claim the free-trader systems. It was not until that final season of the pirate actions that Monsignor Horatio understood his error."

Instead of softening, Bran's expression hardened. "Another media recast of despicable truth."

She reached with her free hand to cup his jaw. "Mayhap. But according to Lorelie, Horatio orchestrated the Governing Council support of Monsignor Lucius' armada to redeem his honor. The same reason he joined the armada in the battle for the Thirteenth System."

Bran's gaze turned inward. "He and William fought well during the maze melee when we confronted Sadico. They did not flee when they could have."

Turning his face, he pressed his lips into her palm.

Encouraged, she continued, "If Monsignor Horatio had not supported the Raven Codicil in the Thirteenth System's Charter, it would not have been included."

She could almost see his mind sifting her words. The controversial provision allied the Thirteenth System with the Eleventh and Twelfth in prohibiting indenture. When added to the elimination of Matahorn control of the supply depots, it created the opportunity for the Eleventh, Twelfth, and Thirteenth systems to form a significant commerce and political bloc. An alliance that would benefit the free-traders and be detrimental to Matahorn's power in the region.

His frown faded, and his eyes warmed. Capturing her hand, he pressed his lips to her knuckles. "The Matahorn legacy in the free-trader systems is a dark one, but I will allow that the cartel is not materially worse than any other and its preeminence is not a villain."

Her heart lifted. "A fair and reasonable response."

"You could not be more different from my wife, but you share one trait." His eyes darkened as a tender smile emerged. His thumbs stroked her wrists. "She too could turn me away from dwelling on darkness and into the light."

Her heart thrilled at his words, and the last wound from her failed consort alliance closed. "You could not be more different from Evander. I far prefer your occasional taciturn behavior to his glib charm. "

His smile broadened. "It is well since it is likely to occur again." His fingers trailed from her wrists to her shoulders, "What must I do to convince you to leave Blue on the sofa and join me in the bedchamber?"

Tilting her head, she leaned in. "You could start with a kiss."

**

Bran feathered his lips over Adriana's, testing her response. Her lips parted, inviting him in. Relief blended with desire at her response. He was becoming addicted to her taste, the vibrant pliancy of her form as she pressed against him, her fingers clasping the back of his neck. Needing more intimate contact, he pressed her into the cushions, the pillowy softness of her breasts against his chest hardening his shaft.

Her arms tightened, and her hips shifted, encouraging further onslaught. He lifted her hip, settling her more firmly.

With an annoyed yelp, Blue abandoned the sofa.

Laughing softly, Adriana ended the kiss. "I forgot she was there."

Her eyes smoldered with desire; her lips delightfully swollen. The loosened collar of her tunic offered a tantalizing glimpse of her throat. Her fingernails scraped the nape of his neck, sending an erotic pulse straight to his groin. Her eyes widened as she felt the evidence of his desire. "You have convinced me."

"Convinced you?"

She tilted her head toward the bedchamber.

***

Bran was even more appealing unclothed, his rangy build elegant with defined muscle, his tan fading to milk and honey at his chest. Even marred by bruises, the sight stirred her. His amber eyes darkened to cognac with passion. When his hands dropped to his trouser fasteners, her desire pulsed, taking her breath and making her clumsy.

His half smile held amusement and promise as she fumbled to remove her bra. When he stepped free of his trousers, his shaft thick and rising, she gave up and pulled the offending garment over her head.

With a warm chuckle, he grasped her waist, his hands hard but gentle as he urged her onto the bed. "You are more lovely than I imagined."

"I-imagined?"

With an affirming sound, he lowered her against the pillows. "Fantasized might be a better word."

His lips grazed hers, making her senses tingle. He deepened the kiss, his tongue teasing hers, the sensuous contact turning her languid. His fingers trailed along her ribs to her waist and then hips, leaving arousal in their wake. Capturing her briefs, he tugged. His lips traced a heated path between her breasts and along her hip as he pulled the scrap of cotton free of her legs.

His shoulders pushed between her thighs that fell open without resistance, revealing her slick cleft. "Far better than my fantasies."

He pressed his lips against her, and bliss rocketed through her. Instead of continuing, he kissed his way back up to lips. Bracing his forearms, he pressed the hard length of his erection against her. The warm smooth satin of his buttocks was solid beneath her palms. She flexed her fingers and he groaned. His mouth left hers to wander until it captured the tight tip of one breast.

"Bran!" She tunneled her fingers through his hair. The shaggy mass had tempted her for months.

Warm lips and hot breath wove a seductive path down her belly. Dragging her hands along his back, she explored the contours, heat, and strength. Her fingers clinging to his shoulders when he reached his goal, his shoulders between her open thighs.

With teeth, lips, and tongue he tormented her most sensitive flesh. Her hands fisted in the sheets to contain the exquisite pleasure until it became impossible and ecstasy exploded through her. The delight ebbed, breath returning with the sensation of Bran's lips teasing the delicate spot where her neck joined her shoulder—a magical zone that brought her to awareness and reignited fading desire.

His head lifted, revealing eyes hot with desire, a face tight with passion. "You make the most beautiful sounds during release."

Sounds? Me? "For truth?"

His smile was all pleased male. "Let us see if you will do it again."

She doubted that was possible but tilted her pelvis in invitation.

His expression becoming intent, he slid an arm under her thigh, lifting her knee toward her shoulder. The tip of his shaft teased her entrance, the glancing contact rousing her senses. His hard length slid in, caressing delicate internal muscles. Tightening her pelvis, she relished the slow thrust filling her. With the same deliberate slowness, he withdrew and plunged within—each drag and thrust building her passion anew.

His eyes locked with hers, filled with emotion beyond description. "Infinite."

"Infinite?"

"When I move in you, we breathe as one. The wonder of it touches infinity. Eternity."

Her breath caught, and wonder filled her at words more exquisite than this pleasure. She rolled her hips, lips parting. "You are wondrous."

His mouth claimed hers, locking them from lips to pelvis and she could feel her senses expanding.

He released her lips and pressed deeper. Withdrew. Thrust again. Until the tender penetration was not enough. Wrapping her free leg around his waist, she bucked against him. "More. Harder."

Releasing her leg, he shifted position, grasping her hips to tilt her for his pleasure. With increasing speed and force he powered into her until her vision clouded, and another wave of bliss crashed over her. With a guttural cry, he spasmed within her.

6. Toxin and Terrier

Sevenday 32, Day 2

Bran's eyes opened in the dim chamber. Set to brighten slowly, the chamber mimicked dawn, the light not yet bright enough to wake Adriana. She had fallen asleep curled on his chest, but sometime in the night moved away. Facedown on the pillows, she had kicked free of the bedding, the graceful line of her back begging for his lips, the plump mounds of her ass tempting him to nip.

A bruise near her hip caught his attention, the purple smudge marring the tawny expanse. From the color, it had occurred in the crash or soon after.

Her sleepy voice asked, "What are you looking at?"

"You." He lifted his gaze to meet sleepy dark eyes. "You are so very lovely."

She yawned and rolled onto her back, with a wry expression. "Flatterer."

She was correct, *lovely* was a weak compliment at best.

"I regret I have no gift with words." He racked his brain. "Exquisite?"

She ducked her head, her voice small. "I am not tall and slender and elegant."

What says she? He could think of but one woman who met that description, his wife. "Odette?"

She shrugged, reaching to pull up the covers.

It would be easy to let it go. More comfortable for him but not fair to her. He rolled toward her, catching her shoulders to spoon her against him. "Her family disapproved of me."

***

Surrounded by Bran's warmth, Adrian tried to make sense of his words. She had been a fool to mention Odette, but instead of turning taciturn, Bran was sharing his past. She placed her hand over his. "Why would they disapprove of you?"

"She was well-educated, and I was an itinerant freighter pilot scrambling for each new contract. They wanted someone who could offer her more security."

Turning, she searched his expression, relaxing when she found serenity mixed with a hint of amusement at remembered conflict. "How did you meet?"

"At a gallery. I was lured within by a painting, and it turned out to be one of hers." He turned on his back, pulling her with him. "I was but thirty and she was in her twenties. We were both so young.

"It started as a sevenday flirtation. I had a contract that took me away for a season. She sent alerts every day. By the time I returned, I could not imagine life without her. Her family protested, but they could not stop her. If I had been a little older, I might have understood her parents' concerns, but I was convinced I would find a way to prove myself."

She recalled his mention of joining Raleigh. "You were proved correct. You joined Captain Raleigh and invented the DOP-C."

"She believed I could do anything, so I did too." His fingers played with hers. "There was also my determination to prove her parents mistaken."

She tried to imagine him two decades gone, young, talented, and so very driven. "What of your family?"

"I had lost my parents by then and have little contact with my few cousins." He sighed. "She was a vibrant spirit. Her energy filled all the empty spaces."

She sounded wonderful—and nothing like Adriana's contained,

analytical temperament. "You still love her."

"She will always have a place in my heart." His arm tightened on her waist. "But it was a long time ago. In the words of an Eleventh System poet, 'The past is a lesson. The future is a hope. Only the moment is real.'"

He released her fingers to lift her chin. "In the past decade, only one woman has stirred me, and she is in my arms."

He was remarkable. The Matahorn dossier had included minimal data on his early years. She had assumed that as Raleigh's partner in Phoenix Enterprises and well-regarded by Monsignor Lucius and his consort, Bran had come from the upper levels of the free-trader systems. Instead, he had forged a path through trial with skill, determination, and honor. It had taken courage for Bran to share so much. She would do no less. "I joined the *Nightingale* fleeing humiliation, certain that the First System was the pinnacle of our society. In a year, you have shattered a lifetime of bias. You are the most remarkable man I have ever known, and I would rather be in this moment with you than in the finest spire in the First System."

His eyes darkened, and he captured her mouth. Twining her legs with his, she gave herself over to the wonder of his embrace.

***

Bran did not consider pride one of his failings, but Adriana's words left him feeling capable of legendary feats. Seeking the object of his desire, he found her in the sitting area.

Flushed with embarrassment, Adriana shook the throw over the waste-disposal unit, attempting to dislodge the clinging white hairs. "Bran, I beg your pardon. I should have thought."

She was adorable, and he had no desire to see her upset. "Peace, woman. Blue may be an ancients' genetic miracle, but she is yet a dog. They shed. I should have thought to remove the throw, but for truth, I was preoccupied by far more important matters. "

Approaching her back, he wrapped his arms around her waist,

nuzzling her neck. "Well worth it. And it launders without difficulty."

With a final shake of the throw, she leaned into his caress. "I knew I erred to let her onto my bed. We will never keep her off the furniture, now."

He delighted in the scent of his cleansing products on her skin. "You sound as if you wish to keep her on the *Nightingale*."

She sighed and turned to face him. "It is foolish. Somehow, I keep forgetting she is native to Bright Star Deuce."

Bran did not think her foolish and was about to voice it when his slate chimed. "That is the captain." With regret, he released her to grasp his slate. "Sinead's stealth!"

Adriana was at his side. "What is it?"

Struggling between horror and excitement, he turned the slate. "The chief medic demands your presence."

She scanned the alert and shook her head. "It is impossible. We know it was a plant-based toxin that killed the samples. If the mechanic died of similar symptoms, she did not catch a disease from Blue."

He grabbed his satchel. "Or she died of the same poison. That mechanic was training to maintain the DOP-Cs."

***

Chief Medic Imogen was a handsome woman in her mid-fifties. Distant kin to Monsignor Horatio, she and Adriana enjoyed a cordial professional relationship, and pleasant, if cool, personal acquaintance. A woman of serene competence, her expression held uncharacteristic displeasure. Her dark eyes were hard, her olive-toned cheeks flushed. "I have been waiting most of a period. Have you no notion of urgency?"

When Raleigh followed Adriana and Bran into the medic's office, Imogen's eyes narrowed. "Captain, thank you for joining us. If what I suspect is true, I will need to institute a quarantine."

Adriana shook her head. "It is not what you think. A plant toxin killed my samples. And probably the mechanic. There is no unknown disease leaping from the indigenous species to our people."

Raleigh dropped into the nearest chair. "I am responsible for the delay. We needed time to determine how much contact you had with the murder victim."

"Murder?" The medic echoed, fixing her gaze on the captain. "Contact? You suspected me?"

"We needed to be certain. We have a saboteur aboard and they killed the mechanic."

"What say you? How? You say it was a toxin, but I found naught."

Bran motioned Adriana into the other chair. "Adriana, if you would?"

Pulling out her slate, Adriana provided the results of her tests and evidence that the toxin was plant-based. Frowning, Imogen turned to her techno array. "A moment. That toxin may have killed your samples, but the similar symptoms do not mean it killed our mechanic. If this is present in our dead mechanic, it *is* murder."

Bran made a soft sound. "Scientists and certainty."

Imogen ignored him, her fingers flitting over the controls. "Adriana, join me if you please."

It did not take long. The same toxin Adriana found in the snake was present in the dead woman. "What do you think? When was she poisoned?"

Imogen pursued her lips. "No later than seventh bell last eve. Mayhap as early as midday." She turned from the techno array as Adriana returned to her chair. "It had to be someone from your team, mine, or the botanists."

The medic was sharp. Her kinship ties with the Margovian preeminence may have aided her assignment to the *Nightingale*, but she was well-qualified for the role.

Adriana looked at Raleigh. "Everyone on my team has been to the planet's surface and could have sourced a poisonous plant. It would not be that difficult to smuggle it on board."

Imogen nodded. "As with mine."

Bran made a sound of disagreement. "We should start with the mechanic. Either the saboteur arranged for her to damage the DOP-C, or they spent sufficient time with her to elicit the information."

Imogen's eyes narrowed. "That is why you needed to know how much contact I had with her. I have the skills to make poison, but not sabotage a DOP-C. Do you think she was a dupe or complicit?"

Bran shrugged. "Either way, she became a liability."

Adriana's heart lurched. "Blue. If I had not brought Blue aboard, they might not have used the poison."

Bran shook his head. "The mechanic would still be dead, only by other means. As it is, they have given us our first real lead. It had to be someone well known to the dead woman, with the ability to identify and conceal poisonous plants."

Imogen's lips twisted. "Where is Security Chief Lochan in this? Why is he not in this chamber?"

"We can trust no one."

Imogen bristled. "You would question Lochan's honor? His loyalty?"

Raleigh held up a hand. "For truth, I find it difficult to believe he is another Sadico, but he is in the ideal position to orchestrate this mess. Until we have incontrovertible evidence of his innocence, I dare not trust him."

The medic opened her mouth and the door pinged. It recessed to reveal the man under discussion. In his mid-forties, Lochan was average height, and lean in the manner of one who is all sinew and muscle. He kept his swarthy head shaved but maintained a tightly trimmed black beard. His dark gray eyes were sharp under heavy brows. "It appears our mechanic was murdered."

Raleigh's eyebrows lifted and Lochan made a scoffing sound. "If she had died from some unknown pathogen brought from the planet by that dog, you would not be sitting in chamber with two potential carriers." He looked around. "Where is the animal?"

Bran answered, "Sealed in my quarters. But how did you make the leap from it not being Blue to murder?"

Lochan's jaw hardened. "I am not a lackwit. There is a saboteur on the *Nightingale*."

Raleigh sighed. "And while unlikely, that saboteur could be you."

The security chief went rigid.

"Incontrovertible proof?" Imogen interrupted. "We may have that. We know the mechanic was poisoned between midday and seventh bell. Lochan, can you prove you were nowhere near the woman?"

"I can."

Bran sighed. "That does not rule out Lochan having someone else administer the poison."

Imogen snorted. "How many confederates do you think are involved? For Lochan to be behind this, he needed to suborn someone with knowledge of poisons, seduce this poor mechanic, have someone tamper with medical equipment, and who knows what else. And if he is killing off his loose ends, we should be knee-deep in bodies."

Raleigh barked a laugh. "You are right. Lochan, my apologies. I have allowed paranoia to cloud my judgment."

Lochan's shoulders softened and he shook his head. "I had Bran on the suspect list until the DOP-C crash." He moved to the desk and propped himself on the edge. "So far, we are certain that someone has been sabotaging our efforts and that they are escalating. First the DOP-C, and now murder by poison. That suggests someone from the medical, botany, or zoology teams. What else do you know?"

It was not much, and after a few pointed questions, Lochan concluded, "Whoever it is needs someplace to store and refine an uncatalogued plant."

Bran's eyes narrowed. "Or miscataloged as indigestible rather than toxic."

Startled, Adriana asked, "How do you know about Clarence and the river snails?"

"I reviewed his records. I can account for his movements during several incidents, so he is not our saboteur, but you are correct; he is incompetent. He will be dismissed as soon as we can put him on a militia transport bound for Fortuna."

Lochan made an impatient gesture. "Explain. Why is this important?"

Imogen answered, "The river snails? First, it could have as readily been miscataloged as consumable, and death could have resulted. Second, toxins often have medical uses. Classing it as indigestible would have put it at the bottom of the list of items for medical review."

He looked at Bran. "You have ruled out Lt. Clarence but think someone else might have deliberately miscataloged a poisonous plant to keep it hidden?"

"Rimon's dungeons!" The words were out before Adriana thought. At the shocked stares, she ran nervous fingers through her curls. "I know why the DOP-C crashed. It was about me. Or rather something I was about to do. Clarence is incompetent, but we are all working long bells to make up for lost time. After the snail incident, zoology increased validation checks. We caught two other errors. I was going to propose that all departments implement similar protocols."

Bran scowled. "Who knew about this?"

"I mentioned it to my team," Adriana replied, beginning to feel like a lackwit. "Clarence is enamored of the Serengeti botanist."

Lochan snorted. "She is among the most pursued females on the *Nightingale*. What would she see in Clarence?"

"I was surprised she seemed to encourage his interest, but since he was so well connected within Blooded Dagger..." Adriana trailed off with an embarrassed shrug. Had she not been so biased, she might have seen through Clarence months ago.

Lochan frowned. "Demon scat. She is manipulating him."

Raleigh's expression hardened. "Mayhap not only him. Had she much contact with our murdered maintenance tech?"

***

Cyclops piss. Bran opened and closed his fists, attempting to release his frustration. From his expression, Lochan was no happier with the unsuccessful search. Nothing had been found in the botanist's quarters that implicated her in the sabotage, and no trace of poison.

Imogen's review revealed the botanist had miscataloged poison. When dried, the small yellow berries darkened to brown. Crushed, three or four berries were sufficient to kill an adult, and with a mild enough taste to be introduced to food without detection.

Locating it in her quarters was a low-probability play, but it would have provided the evidence needed for interrogation.

Sealing the door, Lochan said, "Reviewing the monitor records will be tedious. I propose we start with the most serious incidents."

"Agreed. A day on either side? If there is no sign of Clarence or the botanist, move on?"

Lochan thought for a moment and then nodded. "If we find naught, we can each take a suspect and work backward."

***

Adriana sent the wadded cleansing cloth sliding across the floor. Ears and tail up, Blue chased the improvised ball, pouncing before it disappeared beneath the desk. It had required a quarter period before Blue understood the game, but now she was all in. Her faux prey between her teeth, Blue pranced across the floor and dropped it by Adriana's knees. It was not the level of exercise the terrier needed, but it was better than naught. Picking it up, she tossed it in an arc. Blue leaped, snatching it out of the air.

"Good girl!"

Blue brought it back, crouching in anticipation of the next toss. With a flick of her wrist, Adriana sent it flying toward the cabinets. A chime punctuated her movement. Knowing it could be Bran or Lochan, she rose and reached for her slate.

With an apologetic smile, she looked down at the dog. "So much for playtime, Blue."

Blue's hopeful gaze followed Adriana as she settled behind her techno array. With a sigh, Blue settled in a corner, resting her muzzle on the improvised toy.

With no evidence against the botanist, Adriana would need to review the zoology monitor records in search of the poisoner. She was all but certain it was Clarence. If they could find proof, they could use it to force him to implicate his confederate. It would not take much. Imogen had located the record where the botanist had misclassified the poison. If they could find evidence of Clarence using it as a poison, the botanist could not claim misclassification was a mistake.

Three separate monitors recorded the area where the snake remains were stored. A full dozen covered the live specimen area, and there were another four where the specimens' food was prepared. With a few taps, she had the images of the first animal to die.

***

Bran understood why many found the botanist attractive. She could have served as model for a Sinead effigy with her sculpted cheekbones, long straight nose, deep-set eyes, full lips, and tall, well-toned build. The woman had never moved him. Had some deep instinct recognized her lack of honor? Her callous disregard for any needs but her own?

Bran started reviewing the periods before he entered the sabotaged DOP-C. Free-traders were not prone to warrior paranoia and did not activate monitors unless the DOP-C was in flight. From the maintenance record, the mechanic had accessed the craft the day before it crashed. Tracing her movements backward, he found her exiting the botanist's quarters.

A review of what occurred in those quarters proved that the tech was enamored of the botanist but provided no evidence of collusion. With a sigh, he continued to trace the mechanic's movements.

***

Adriana leaned back in her chair and scowled at the reviewer screen. She had two records of Clarence feeding the live specimens the day before they died. In both, he managed to keep his hands hidden. Given his attitude, and refusal to perform mundane tasks, she should have been suspicious when he did not balk at feeding the animals. At the time, she had been pleased, thinking his affection for the animals indicated he was not as objectional as she believed.

The door chimed. Glancing over, she saw Clarence's face in the window. It was the third time in the past period. He was going to harass her until he had what he wanted.

Deciding it was better to deal with him, she released the door lock. As soon as it started to open, she realized her reviewer displayed the monitor record of Clarence feeding the animals. Turning her back to him, she blocked the screen while hiding her work.

"What is it you require," she asked, pivoting the chair to face him across the desk.

He held two cups in his hands and offered one to her. "Tea?"

Even without knowing that he was enamored of a poisoner, she would have wondered at his sudden desire to seek her approval. Taking the cup, she lifted the lid and blew on the liquid. "It is a little hot."

She set it down and leaned back. She did not know what Clarence was about, but she was certain Bran should know he was here. "Do you have the report on the specimen movements?"

"As it happens, I wished to discuss my assignment queue." He took a long sip of tea. "It seems cool enough."

She was not drinking that tea. Trying for casual, she replied, "Let me take a look."

Two taps would have Bran on the way.

Clarence's arm flew across the desk, hitting her shoulder and knocking her chair into the wall. Stunned, she had struggled free of the chair, determined to reach the door into the lab. With far more strength than she could have imagined, he grabbed her from behind and wrapped his forearm around her throat.

***

At Lochan's sharp humming sound, Bran looked up from his reviewer. "Did you find something?"

"Remember that incident where meteorology lost half a month of data from a device failure?"

Excitement fizzed in his veins. "And?"

Lochan turned his reviewer. "Our botanist visiting the meteorology lab."

On the screen, one of the meteorologists was sprawled in a chair braced against the equipment console. His tunic was open, and their suspect was riding his lap in an unmistakable and carnal manner. One of her hands pawed the console.

Lochan tapped his console and the image enlarged to show a slender metal rod in her fingers. It flashed white for a second and the console flickered. Lochan hummed again. "Power surge device. Disrupted the technologistics and fried a section of data storage."

"Sinead's spite! It is a pest pulsar."

Lochan's attention snapped onto him. "You recognize the device?"

"Each DOP-C has two. They produce a high-frequency tone that clears small animals from ten paces around a campsite." He could feel his teeth grind. "It also uses a short, low-power burst of electromagnetic energy to discourage reptiles and insects."

"Dangerous camping device that can disrupt systems."

"It does not. But it would not be difficult to modify it for that purpose. That burst of light indicates it was altered."

"A change that a DOP-C mechanic could accomplish?"

"Any competent mechanic as well as any of the *Nightingale* engineers." He rubbed the tense muscles in his neck. "Adriana can change out a vistrite controller."

Lochan huffed. "Not that it matters. We have the monitor record of the botanist employing it to destroy meteorological data. More than enough to incarcerate and question her."

"I should have Adriana look for her in the zoology records." He picked up his slate. "It could be she used the device for the equipment malfunction that turned that set of genetic samples to goop."

"The more evidence the better." He stopped tapping instructions and rose. "I will report to the captain."

Bran frowned at this slate. "Adriana is not responding."

"Could be in the freshener." Lochan leaned back over his console. "Odd, the monitor in her office is off."

"She has had it on command lockout since we returned."

Lochan straightened and turned to the weapons vault. "Not locked. *Off.*"

Bran crossed the chamber in two strides, reaching past the pistols for a rifle.

Lochan's hand landed on his forearm. "Too dangerous."

The *Nightingale*'s hull could survive multiple blasts, but a missed shot could destroy sensitive equipment with a glancing hit. Bran shook him off. "I hit my targets."

***

Adriana fought the iron-hard forearm cutting off her breath. Her fingers dug for purchase against the durable uniform fabric. She kicked against his shins. Clarence tightened his grip, throwing her against the desk, pinning her facedown. His voice hissed in her ear. "You will drink the tea if I must force it down your throat."

Her lungs burning, and vision dimming, she groped around the desk, seeking a weapon.

Clarence screamed and released her. Scrabbling away, she fell to the floor, Clarence shrieking behind her. With hands and knees, she propelled herself toward the door, reaching it as it recessed. Booted feet appeared and then strong hands lifted her. Bran's voice rumbled. "Are you injured? What did he do?"

Gasping, she clung to him, burying her face in his chest. Forcing words past her aching throat, she croaked, "Poison. Tea."

The screaming had turned to moans. Turning in Bran's arms she could see Lochan bent over behind the desk, but nothing of Clarence. A white form leaped onto the desk. Blue turned her bloody muzzle toward Adriana.

Behind her, she heard Govind gasp. "Five Warriors protect us."

Lochan looked over his shoulder at the man. "Send for the medics."

Swallowing shock, Adriana attempted to see over Lochan. "What did Blue do?"

Bran pulled her back. "Savaged his shoulder and an ear. I am surprised she did not tear out his throat."

"Had me in a choke hold. She could not reach."

Bran's arms tightened. "Good dog."

7. Star Bred Terrier

Sevenday 32, Day 3

Adriana opened her eyes to find Bran, propped on pillows, perusing his slate. Rubbing sleep from her eyes, she asked, "Aught new?"

He lifted his eyes, a warm smile forming. "Good morning."

She garbled "good morning" past a yawn, then repeated the greeting, pleased her voice was no longer a croak. She ran a finger along the sealant that the medics had applied to minimize the bruising, finding it dry.

Bran's smile deepened. "It has gone gray. It will rinse off when you shower. How do you feel?"

Sitting up, she swung her legs over the side of the bed. "Well. What of Clarence?"

"The medics repaired his shoulder and reattached his ear. The ear will need cosmetic intervention, and it will be three months before he has full mobility and strength. Assuming he lives that long."

"What say you?" Unable to locate her tunic, she grabbed Bran's from the floor. "Did he confess?"

"No. He and the botanist continue to claim they were seduced by the other." Bran set aside his slate. "But there was poison in that tea, and we have a monitor record that shows him using the modified pulsar to turn those experiments to goop."

The tunic did not quite cover her thighs. "I cannot imagine it will take long to get one of them to confess."

Heat entered Bran's gaze as it wandered over her. "We will not have the honor. Seigneur Trevelyan ordered both saboteurs onto the next militia transport bound for Fortuna. They will be gone by the time we return from the planet."

She stopped at the door to the freshener, looking back at Bran. "Matahorn agreed to this?"

Bran nodded. "Seconded the order. I suspect both Trevelyan's and Seigneur William's operatives will participate in the interrogation."

She started to say something and stopped. That Seigneur William oversaw Matahorn security-privilege was not well publicized, but she had no cause to be surprised it was well known among the upper levels of Serengeti. "Both Serengeti and Matahorn elicited the truth from despoilers. Do they suspect our saboteurs?"

"Of being despoilers?" Bran shook his head. "But the list of commerce interests that would benefit from slowing exploration of the Thirteenth System is a long one. Discovering who had the resources and audacity to sabotage us is paramount to Bright Star."

The cost of the *Nightingale* was staggering. Add the ancillary expenses from infrastructure to governing council fees, and venture had required the pooling of massive resources. Then there was the cost of defending the Thirteenth System. Everyone on the *Nightingale* knew that the Bright Star principals needed the funds that would come from licensing mining and other rights. The longer exploration dragged out, the more desperate Bright Star would be for funds. Desperate enterprises did not fare well in contract negotiations.

Stepping into the freshener, Adriana mused that whatever commerce interest had set Clarence and his paramour to their tasks would soon be locked out of the Thirteenth System. And while Lucius Mercio had a reputation for ruthlessness, Horatio Margovian was beyond vindictive and controlled the governing council. There would not be much left of the enterprise that instigated the sabotage when those two warriors were done.

***

Bran set the DOP-C on a course for the western edge of the plains. Adriana believed that since Blue had headed in that direction on her own, it was likely the terrier made her home somewhere between their former landing site and where the plains gave way to the arid section bordering the mountains.

"If she heads east, then we know we have gone too far west," Adriana said from behind him. "If she heads west, it will tell us a great deal about her range and the size of the pack's territory."

"Are you so certain she has a pack?"

"Canines are pack creatures, and she is too healthy to be a loner."

He glanced over his left shoulder to find Adriana rubbing the little terrier's ears. In the cargo area, several crates held supplies for three days as well as their travel bags. It was not the romantic getaway Adriana deserved, but Bran was delighted to have a few days alone with her.

The engines hummed as they breached the thermosphere and Bran turned all his attention to the console. All systems stayed functional, the DOP-C descending through gauzy clouds to land in dusty purple, a half mile south of the forest area. He would have preferred to be farther away from the trees and the predators that dwelled in them, but Adriana did not want to be too far south of their original site. In their favor, it was early in the day, not past ninth bell. Whatever nocturnal predators lurked in the trees would not be stirring for bells.

The dusty purple color of the plains was not due to dust. The fibrous purple plants were thinner, growing up through pale gold grass. It made him think of harvest season at home, although according to the meteorologists, this segment of the planet was experiencing early summer.

Next to him, Adriana rubbed some of the stalks between her fingers. "Interesting. It is the color of the grain harvests on Socraide Prime but feels like summer grass. Cool, pliant." She tilted her head, bringing the grass to full light. "It has a pinkish caste. Mayhap some cross-pollination with the heather."

"You were wise to bring some botanical sample cases."

"With both zoology and botany reduced by one, we will need to do more cross-department surveys." Rising, she brushed her hands on the seat of her trousers. "But first, let us see where Blue will lead us."

She looked around. "Blue?"

A sharp bark came from the west, Blue's white muzzle rising out of the surrounding plants. Rolling her shoulders under her pack, Adriana activated her tracker. The palm-sized device held the topography mapping for the area, Blue a glowing white dot against the background. Grinning, she moved after the terrier. "As long as she remains white, we will not need this to follow, but I do want to record her path."

Bran scanned the area for threats. "How certain are you that she will lead us to a pack?"

"She cannot be the only Star Bred terrier on the planet. How would she have been born?"

"Star Bred terrier?"

"If my theory is correct, the ancients bred her kind for stellar travel. And, since I found her, I get to name the breed."

"Not the Adriana Pepys terrier?"

"I did not develop the breed, only discovered it." She shrugged. "Blue and her kind deserve a name in keeping with their origins."

He suspected other zoologists would not be so modest in similar circumstances. He wanted to kiss her. Instead, he reached for her free hand. "Blue, the Star Bred terrier. A sevenday gone, I would have thought it the title of an entertainment."

She smiled at him. "Well, Blue is entertaining. And fast. We need to pick up our pace."

Thirty paces ahead, the terrier stopped and turned, giving a sharp bark.

"It appears Blue agrees," he said. "But we should keep to a walk. There could be hidden holes or other hazards."

***

Two bells later and five miles northwest of their landing site, sweat dampened Adriana's tunic and matted the hair at her nape. For all the mild temperatures, the sun was fierce, making her grateful for her wide-brimmed hat and sunshades. After more than a period following Blue, the heather had all but disappeared in favor of grass. The woods were only fifty paces away but had thinned dramatically. There were wide gaps between the trees allowing dark green shrubs to thrive. Even with the dense shrubs, pathways were visible.

Bran held out a hand. "Hold a minute."

Nodding, she reached into her pack for a water vial.

"Blue is heading into the trees." He lifted the distance-viewer hanging from the strap around his neck. "From here, it seems safe enough. I can make out a couple of game trails, but there is enough sunlight getting through the canopy, I do not think the predators are a threat."

"According to the map, this section of woods is not much more than half a mile wide." She took a swallow, holding the map for his view. "It is the tip between the plains and the arid section before the mountains."

"No water source."

"None that showed up in the topography scans, but the trees could hide a small pool or creek."

A sharp bark from Blue announced her return, hopeful blue eyes on the vial.

Laughing, Adriana crouched and poured water into her palm. "It may be too late to return her to the wild."

Shaking droplets from her muzzle, Blue trotted off toward the trees, making no attempt to reestablish her lead.

Adriana glanced at Bran. "We may be getting close."

Within minutes they were following Blue down a game trail. It was pleasantly cool beneath the trees, the forest floor hard beneath a thin layer of decaying vegetation. Bird song and the soft scuffling of small animals went silent with their passing. Bran's free hand dropped to his pistol.

"It could be Blue," she said.

Bran shook his head. "Birds do not fear creatures that cannot climb."

"Us, then. We are alien invaders. Unknown and therefore dangerous."

"Mayhap. But I do not share your confidence that Blue's pack will accept our presence."

She started to protest and thought better of it. Bran would not use the pistol without provocation.

The soft light brightened ahead, sunlight streaming through the trees making Blue's fur glow. The trees gave way, revealing a clear pool with a rocky ledge on the far side. Beyond the tumbled rocks, she could see the distant mountains rising toward the clear sky. It was beautiful. And perfect for a pack with a clean water source and a ledge that she was certain held caves. It had ready access to the woods and plains for hunting without having to enter the more dangerous sections of the forest.

It was also empty. Where was Blue's pack?

Bran's voice was low. "Can this be it?"

Blue skirted the pond, tail up as she navigated jumbled stones up to the ledge. Shadows moved and then brightened to white revealing another terrier, a third larger than Blue. With a *yip*, Blue licked the other dog's muzzle, tail wagging.

"That is the alpha."

Intelligent blue eyes turned to the sound of Adriana's voice. Its snout lifted, nostrils twitching. It cocked its head much as Blue had done at their first meeting. Without warning, it leapt past Blue, springing down the rocks without visibly touching. Reaching the pond edge, it slowed, walking forward, head lowered, tail moving in a slow glide. Bending, Adriana offered her hand, fingers curled and knuckles outward. The alpha came forward. Sniffed. Backed up.

"Come on, little alpha. I will not harm you."

It eased forward, sniffed again.

She brushed its jaw with her knuckles. "Pretty . . ." she canted her head for a better view. "Boy. You are a pretty boy."

It pushed its head against her knuckles. Accepting the invitation, Adriana rubbed its ears. When it accepted the caress, she used both hands and its eyes slit with pleasure. "Bran, come closer; let him get your scent."

The terrier's eyes opened, but he did not move away. He sniffed Bran and then accepted one of Bran's hands in the place of Adriana's. Straightening, she let Bran continue to pet the alpha. Blue was still on the far side of the pond, watching. "Blue?"

With a doggy grin, she bounded down the rocks and back to Adriana.

The alpha's low growl had Blue skirting Bran to reach Adriana and Bran starting to straighten.

"Keep petting him. The growl was canine for *mine*. He is not about to share your attention with Blue."

"Are they it? These two?"

"No. Look." On the ledge, another five terriers appeared. Four more crouched among the tumbled rocks above the ledge, no doubt near entrances to their caves. "With Blue and the alpha, eleven. Maybe one or two more out hunting. It is a sizable pack."

"What now?"

"We make friends."

"How?"

"I have four lures in my pack. A few of the plains rodents should make a decent start."

***

"Are you sure this is wise?" Bran asked. He carried two lures squirming with ground squirrels. "I thought we did not wish to disrupt their behavior patterns."

Adriana shifted her lure, the furball it contained frozen in a protective sphere. "Star Bred terriers are not wild creatures. They are hard-wired to want our companionship."

"Is that why you offered Blue a piece of nutrition bar?" While they waited for the lures to populate, they returned to the Star Bred Terrier den, settling on the far side of the ledge to consume a midday meal of nutrition bars. When offered a piece, Blue sniffed it, then licked it before turning her muzzle away in disgust.

The alpha had appeared and showed a similar disdain before returning to the ledge to doze in the sun. According to Adriana it was normal for canines in the wild to be active dusk to dawn. If Adriana had not been out at dusk that first night, it may have been months before they discovered the terriers.

Adriana glanced at the dog trotting by her side. "I was curious to see how she would react to processed food."

"It was cruel of the ancients to abandon them."

"It may not have been intentional. They could have died here at the outset of the Anarchy."

"We have found nothing that resembles a settlement, despite speculation."

Several ancients' scholars had petitioned to explore the planets for potential ruins. Only the first three systems held ancients' remnants. None had been found in any of the systems discovered by the Five Warriors or their descendants.

"We still have almost half of this continent to survey." Adriana gestured toward Blue. "The terriers may have traveled from their original location, but I doubt they crossed oceans or the stellar expanse."

Bran chuckled, wishing he had a free hand to take hers.

When they reached the clearing, Adriana continued to the edge of the pond before lowering her lure. By the time he had his lures next to hers, the alpha had appeared. It sniffed at a ground squirrel and gave an eager bark. More terriers appeared, either drawn by the alpha or the scent of prey.

Adriana tugged Bran's arm. "Let us move back toward the trees. When I release the lures, we do not want to be in the way."

With eleven dogs to three small mammals, Bran expected fighting. Instead, there seemed to be some form of hierarchy and organization. The hunt was brief, and the last three to eat stripped the carcasses.

"Interesting," Adriana murmured. "I wondered about that."

"About what?"

"They are not dirty. They licked their muzzles clean of mud, but there is no dirt from the hunt. That slick feeling to Blue's fur. Engineered to stay clean?"

"If they got muddy, the chameleon effect would not work."

She nodded. "I wonder if it also serves to mask their scent?"

"Research for another day. We need to return to the DOP-C before dark."

***

Better provisioned for camping this time, Bran activated the portable cooker. The sun setting over the mountains was spectacular and the properly used pest pulsar had cleared the area around the DOP-C. They could not safely slumber outside, but at least they could enjoy an evening meal.

Blue gave the cooker an interrogative sniff and then flopped into the grass. She had whined and yipped at the pest pulsar but had not run off. He held no doubt that the terrier would be returning to the *Nightingale*.

At the sound of a soft step, he turned to smile at Adriana. She had pulled her tunic free from her trousers and loosened the top fasteners, revealing a hint of cleavage. Her throat was unmarked. No hint of huskiness lingered in her voice. Clarence should consider himself fortunate that Blue got to him before Bran.

She held up a small container and two cups. "Fortuna green wine. Not ideal with stew, but I thought we deserved the treat."

Smiling, he rose. "You are brilliant."

Taking the cups and container, he set them on the small table before pulling her into his embrace. With a soft sound, she melted against him, her lips feathering against his neck. "I could stand this way all night, but you would miss the sunset."

With a soft laugh, she stepped free and claimed a camp chair. Blue went to her, pushing against her shins until Adriana complied with ear fondles. "She deserves all the petting."

"She does," he agreed, taking the other seat and pouring wine. "Clarence clearly underestimated her ferocity."

"I doubt he saw her. She was asleep in a corner and blended with the floor." Adriana tilted her cup in a salute. "Although, I admit, I underestimated Clarence. I had no notion he was so strong or could move so fast."

"He is a warrior. They revere martial arts."

She gazed at the mountains where the sky was deepening to indigo shot with violet and gold. "He kept fit. Evander was the same. But there is naught lethal about Evander. I let Clarence's incompetence in the lab lead me to believe he was incompetent in all."

He did not like the way her mood was darkening. Reaching for her, he threaded their fingers together. "Enough of that traitor. What are your thoughts about tomorrow? Do we return to the pack?"

"If the alpha will allow it, I would like to give him a tracker. Mayhap the entire pack. And, with your aid, a few monitors in the trees."

The cooker chimed. Lifting their joined hands, he pressed his lips to her knuckles before releasing her.

***

The simple briefs and tank Adriana used for slumber were not seductive, but the ice-blue flattered her complexion. But then, she was hoping that she would not be wearing them for long. Exiting the freshener, she found Bran on the camp bed, propped against pillows, the sheet pooled around his waist revealing his solid chest and abs. Was he wearing briefs? Even if he was, if she had her will, he would not be for long.

His gaze narrowed as his welcoming smile turned into a grin of anticipation. "You are beyond enticing."

He pulled back the covers in invitation and, in the process, revealed his swelling length. Eager to explore him, she crawled onto the bed, sliding down until she could tongue his shaft.

She wanted to give the same exquisite pleasure she had received. She lifted her eyes to find his head thrown back, eyes closed. "Bran, tell me."

The fingers in her hair fisted. "Good. So good."

Her heart swelled even as she bit back frustration at the nonanswer. "What will please you?"

He groaned, his eyes slitting. "All. What you wish will please me."

8. The Ancients

Sevenday 32, Day 4

Adriana was eager for the day's adventure. Delicate muscles were pleasantly tender from the night's activities and there was nothing like fresh clothes to make camping a joy rather than a trial.

Bran was waiting outside the DOP-C, his pack on his shoulders. "Ready?"

Adding sunshades to protect her eyes, she nodded. "Where is Blue?"

A white blur darted from the heather with her muzzle open in a doggy smile. Adriana smiled at Bran. "I guess we are ready."

With a deft motion, he sealed the DOP-C and they set out for the pack den. Within fifty paces, it became clear that Blue had another destination. Instead of northwest, they were heading almost due west toward the mountains.

Bran slowed. "Adriana?"

Matching his pace, she checked the topography map. "It appears safe enough. Almost flat with no fissures or other hazards. The grassland eventually gives way to an arid region and then there are some rocky slopes and the mountains."

"What of the Star Bred Terriers?"

Halting, she compared their position to the pack den. "If we stay in this direction we can loop back toward the den at midday. There will be more than sufficient bells to set monitors and trackers before dark."

Twenty paces ahead, Blue barked.

Bran chuckled. "She is a determined little thing."

"Terrier character trait," Adriana replied. "Clever, willful, and loyal."

Bran gave her a quick kiss. "Well that explains it."

"Explains what?"

Bran strode away, following Blue. "Why the terriers are drawn to you. Like to like."

Laughing, she followed, pleased more by his teasing than the compliment. The taciturn free-trader of a year gone was turning out to be charming as well as attractive.

A period later, the plains ended in a shallow ledge that dropped half a dozen feet to an arid area of scrub and stones. Blue veered north, following the ledge.

Adriana frowned at the topography map and made a note. "This is the challenge of high-altitude surveys. This ledge was invisible."

"One of the reasons we do the low-altitude grid maps before allowing ground teams," Bran said. "If it were not for Blue, it would have been easy to step out into empty space. I do not relish a sprained or broken ankle."

Frowning at the device, she projected Blue's path. "This is interesting. I think she is bringing us behind the pack den."

Bran peered at the device. "The geologists have not made notes."

"A tangle of stone at the edge of a forest?" She shrugged. "Not really noteworthy."

He scanned the area beyond the ledge. "Maybe a dried riverbed. I wonder if this area is prone to flash flooding?"

"That scrub looks more than a season old, but it is barren in the center. Maybe the water only rises this high on occasion." She turned her attention to following Blue. "If there are flash floods, this ledge probably marks the maximum depth."

"Sinead's stealth." Bran had not moved, the distant viewer focused on the mountain range. "The forest is anomalous, but mayhap." He pivoted toward the south then took a deep breath. "It has the markers."

He dropped the viewer, excitement radiating from him. "We need to return to the DOP-C and contact Nickolas."

"Why? What it is it?"

"I cannot be certain; it could be." He gestured toward the mountains. "Nickolas probably caught a glimpse when he was bringing our repair equipment."

She snatched at his forearm. "You are making no sense. What do you think is in that old riverbed?"

He cupped her face with his free hand. "The markers are here. Plains, a long stretch without vegetation. Mountains. The forest is odd, but the plains are huge."

A *Nightingale* tutorial flashed through her memory. The ultimate goal of Bright Star. The most valuable and scarce substance in the galaxy. Eight centuries since the last deposit was discovered. "Vistrite?"

***

The sleek scarlet flyer skimmed the mountains and descended to the riverbed, its flight path curving south until it disappeared. Even with the distance-viewer, Bran could not keep it in sight. "What does the topography show? How far does this arid strip run?"

Adriana was quiet for a moment, adjusting the device. "One-hundred-twenty miles. It ends at the mouth of that bay. The one that feeds the river down to Socraide's ocean."

"Luck of the First Warrior."

"What say you?"

"Monsignor Lucius." Bran lowered the viewer. It would be at least a quarter period before Nickolas returned. "Not only did he originate Bright Star and the discovery of the first new system in two centuries, but he has also discovered the first vistrite deposit in eight."

"That assumes this is vistrite."

"It would explain the Star Bred terriers. Or at least that we found them here."

Adriana glanced down at Blue. Sprawled in the grass, she lifted her head under Adriana's regard. "True enough. Vistrite was as important to the ancients as it is to us."

A dark speck appeared against the horizon. Bran lifted the viewer, and it became a scarlet dot. "Nickolas."

Adriana inhaled sharply. The dot grew into the sleek flyer. It passed them before it ascended and executed a perfect barrel roll. Bran whooshed out a cheer echoed by Adriana. "Vistrite! We have found Vistrite!"

Sevenday 32, Day 6

Adriana sipped tea, enjoying the morning cool and the quiet of the camp that had been set up to accommodate the geologists. In the day and half since Nickolas confirmed the vistrite deposit, her camping expedition with Bran had morphed into a full geological survey of the arid strip of land running toward the bay. Within a bell of Nickolas' flight, Bran had flown them to the ledge, a hundred meters south of the Star Bred terrier woods. Another DOP-C had landed with the lead geologist, two of her assistants, and a militia guard. Nickolas had brought a second guard before using the flyer to ferry the geologists from one end of the riverbed to the other. He returned the next day and continued the effort before returning to the *Nightingale*.

In between the two DOP-Cs, they had erected a tent with seating and camp cookers. The sides were raised to catch the breeze but would drop to enclose the tent in inclement weather. At the early bell, Adriana was alone with Blue, enjoying the view of the mountains.

The arrival of so many additional crew members meant a loss of privacy. Sleeping next to Bran lacked its former intimacy, what with a geologist snoring in the second bed. Nor had she retained Bran's undivided attention.

Before the geologists arrived, Bran assisted her with the monitors installation at the pack area. Once the new arrivals had made camp,

Bran's duty was to the vistrite. But he had not ignored the requirements of her duty, assigning her a militia guard. Accompanied by the guard, she had managed to implant Blue's pack with trackers and collect enough samples to keep zoology and botany occupied for a sevenday.

For truth, in the past sevenday, Bran had proven more supportive and committed to her than Evander had managed in seven years. Despite his misgivings, Bran had supported her exploration after the crash. He defended her accidental acquisition of Blue to Captain Raleigh. He even let Adriana's pet nestle in his favorite throw. Without the need to protect Blue, he might not have invited them to his quarters that night, and they might never have shared the revelations that made their growing intimacy possible. Adriana joined the *Nightingale* to run away from failure, but what she had found was even more wonderful than vistrite.

Bran emerged from the DOP-C, his eyes brightening at the sight of tea and a morning meal waiting for him. They would have a few minutes alone before the rest of the camp woke. He nodded at the monitor device in her hand as he lifted his cup. "Anything of note?"

"Blue's pack appears to claim a twenty-mile area from the ledge to a few meters beyond where she found me that first night."

"Is that important?"

"Interesting. Had we crashed a mile further east, we might not have met Blue."

He reached down to pet the dog. "Monsignor Lucius is not the only one with Luck of the First."

She nodded. "Without Blue and that snake, we might yet be seeking our saboteurs."

All humor fled; he straightened, his hands reaching for her. "Without Blue, that snake might have been your death. I will protect her with all I have."

His intense expression and embrace were as clear as if it were spoken; he referred to Adriana as well as Blue. Taking a deep breath, she let her emotions show on her face. "Without Blue, I might still be more focused on the First System than the Thirteenth. Where we came from rather than where we are."

His eyes lit up. "Where we are is a bit crowded. I will be glad to get back to the *Nightingale* where I can have you to myself."

Warmth flooded her at the promise, and she found herself smiling. "I will need to forage for Blue before we leave. Do you think Captain Raleigh will allow her to run in the hydroponic garden? She will need the exercise, and I cannot think of another area where she will not be in the way."

"I am certain he will agree, but you can ask him yourself. He will be here by midday."

The captain's short, coded alert to headquarters reached the beaconed expanse within a half day of Nickolas' flight. By last eve, the *Nightingale* command crew had been inundated with requests for data. The geologists would have a preliminary assessment ready by midday, and the captain wished to inspect the site in person before responding.

"That will give me sufficient bells to set a monitor on the ledge side of the pack's den."

"I will accompany you."

***

Bran regretted how quickly they made the trek to the stones. Between the DOP-C's new location and the lack of sample equipment, it was not even a half period before they reached their destination.

Adriana stared up at the pile of rocks. "Odd, it did not seem so tall from the other side."

"The pool probably hides some of the height," he replied. "Where do you want to place the monitor?"

She looked north and then toward the vistrite deposit where a lone geologist was planting a marker. "The terriers do not seem to go past the ledge, but they do range both north and south." She turned back to the tumble of rocks. "It we set it between those two stones, near the top, it will get visuals in one hundred twenty degrees."

"Is that enough?"

"It must be. When I return, I can bring more monitors and cover the full range." She shrugged out of her pack. "This will not be difficult. The rocks are almost stairs."

Bran watched her clamber up, followed by Blue. The little terrier was insatiably curious and committed to following Adriana wherever she went. Bran looked more closely at the rocks. On the far side of the rocks, where the den and pool were located, the stones were covered with moss and lichen. Here, exposed to the wind, the rocks were scoured clean—save for a few resilient weeds sprouting in cracks that had filled with dirt. He gave the nearest weed an experimental tug. It pulled free, carrying away dirt and revealing surprisingly sharp edges.

Adriana dropped next to him. "What are you looking at?"

"Does this edge seem unnatural to you?"

She followed his gesture, peering at the gap left by the weed. "Could have whatever tumbled these rocks sheered an edge?"

"Mayhap." He turned back toward the deposit where the geologist was climbing into a survey cart. Unlike the zoologists and botanists who covered relatively narrow sections of terrain at a time, the geologists could range for miles. The lightweight carts collapsed to fit in the passenger space of a flyer. Before the DOP-Cs, it had required half of the flyers to drop a geological team on the planet's surface. Raising his arm, Bran gave a shout. The man looked up but did not turn. Bran waved and shouted again, this time catching the geologist's attention. "We will ask an expert."

Leaving the cart at the base of the ledge, the geologist used the seat as a step and, with a hand up from Bran, joined them by the rocks. "What can I do for you, Commander?"

"What do you think of these stones? Are they natural?"

The man's lips twisted in amusement, but he obediently turned to examine the rocks. His smile fading, he ran his fingers over a boulder's surface. Expression intent, he replaced his sunshades with geologist goggles. Bracing his hand on the stones, he moved from one side to another and then lifted his head, examining the higher rocks. "Mulan's mercy."

"What say you?"

The man turned, lifting the goggles. "Commander, this is crevasse stone."

"There is vistrite under these rocks?" It defied everything Bran knew about vistrite deposits.

"No. These stones were quarried. Pulled from the deposit and dumped here." He gestured toward the marker he had set. "I may even know where. The deposit is closer to the surface there than anywhere else."

Adriana looked at the marker. "Why does that make you think this stone was quarried there?"

"We only have the records from Desperation Crevasse to go on, but from surface to the first crystals was between fifty and sixty meters. Down by the camp it is that depth, and at our other sample sites all the way to end. Here it is not more than five meters. I was about to trace the length of the shallow section when the commander shouted."

"Why dump the stones here?"

He shrugged. "We must put the stone somewhere. And it is ideal for building. In Crevasse City, almost every building uses it. Some of those have foundations that predate the Anarchy."

***

Adriana hastened to keep pace with Raleigh, Bran, and the lead geologist as they walked the twelve meters along the ancients' excavation.

Bracing hands on hips, Raleigh stared south toward the far end of the deposit. "Why so short? Why here?"

Bran followed the captain's gaze. "They cannot have intended a settlement?"

Confused, Adriana asked, "Why not? There is plenty of game. Fresh water in the woods."

The master geologist shook her head. "Those woods are part of the reason. Even thirteen hundred years ago they were extensive. At the other end of the deposit there is naught but plains and a freshwater bay. A far better location for a stellar transport site and the city that will grow up around the crevasse."

Adriana glanced back at the stones marking the pack den. A city would not be good for the terriers.

Raleigh frowned at the marker. "They must have had a reason."

Adriana half closed her eyes, trying to imagine the area thirteen hundred years ago. Or more. "We keep dating the ancients' last days on this planet to the start of the Anarchy. But there is no foundation for that. Ancients' artifacts dating back two millennia were found on Rimon Deuce. Scholars suspect they existed centuries before that."

"You think this trench is two thousand years old?"

"Or more." She looked down at her feet. "I recall the visuals from the Rimon Deuce site. It was fascinating. The remnants of buildings were found six and seven meters down. Buried by time."

Raleigh turned to the geologist. "Could Adriana have the answer? They dug to the deposit for samples?"

"Mayhap," she replied, drawing out the word. Her gaze went to the ledge and then the mountains. "We are at the tip of the crevasse. From this point, the deposit separates. Another five meters and there is a ten-foot gap between the two seams. Within a mile there is a five-hundred-meter gap. The gap reaches four miles at the halfway mark before narrowing to connect again at one-hundred-three miles."

"That still does not answer why not excavate at the other end, near the bay?"

"Cyclops slop." Bran slammed a fist into his palm. "Of course."

Ignoring the geologist's gasp at Bran's vulgarity, Raleigh snorted. "What?"

Bran grinned at his friend and partner. "Opportunity canyon on

Redemption. The river is long gone; only the lake remains."

Raleigh laughed. "Two thousand years or more."

The geologist frowned. "I do not understand."

Neither did Adriana and she was glad the other woman asked.

"Opportunity is a massive canyon cut by a river at some point in the distant past. The river is gone, but it retains a lake at its far end. One that was once much bigger."

Of course. Adriana had identified half the answer. While time had buried the ancients' excavation, it had also altered the topography at the far end of the deposit. During the ancients' time, that bay could have covered part of the seam.

The geologist's eyes widened. "I should have thought . . . The ancients' terraforming was far beyond ours. If the other end of the vistrite seam was under water, they would have found a way to reveal it."

Raleigh nodded. "They probably left, intending to return when the vistrite was fully exposed."

Anger lit Adriana's heart. "And left their dogs behind."

Bran squeezed her shoulder. "Not necessarily. If Blooded Dagger needed to wait to settle Deuce, the cartouche would leave an outpost. In the ancients' time, while the planet was terraforming, they would need supplies."

Adriana's anger faded, replaced by compassion. "The Anarchy took hold and there were no more supply transports. The ancients were unable to adapt, but the terriers fared better."

"It seems the most likely explanation."

Raleigh turned to the geologist. "What think you? Relocate to the other end?"

"That is where excavation needs to start." Hands on her hips, the woman faced south, oozing satisfaction. "The third-largest crevasse in the Thirteen Systems. Longer than Desperation Crevasse by three miles. The *Nightingale*'s bonus will be outstanding."

Sevenday 32, Day 7

Bran could feel excitement rushing through every member of the command crew. Even those not on duty had gathered on the bridge to hear the Bright Star governors' response to the vistrite discovery.

Raleigh rose from his chair, slate in hand. "Bran, if you please."

Nodding, Bran configured the communications systems to relay Raleigh's image and voice to every corner of the *Nightingale*.

Raleigh lifted his slate. "The Bright Star governors commend the crew of the *Nightingale* on an accomplishment that will benefit all within the Thirteen Systems."

Bran could feel his shoulders square with pride.

Raleigh's teeth flashed in a smile. "They have also confirmed our bonus. In addition to the lump-sum honor payment, we—or our heirs—will receive royalties on the first decade of vistrite extraction."

It was a warrior's ransom for the command crew. Enough for lifetime financial security for even the most junior crew member. Lochan was the first to break the silence with a resounding, "Bright Star!"

Bran answered with, "*Nightingale!*"

Soon another fifteen voices joined in, filling the chamber with exuberant thunder. Tapping his console, Bran set it to receive communications and the cheers reached deafening proportions. Raleigh allowed it for a few breaths before signaling silence.

Whatever divisions may have existed when the DOP-C crashed, Bran was certain that the *Nightingale* crew was fully united.

Raleigh clasped his hands behind his back and lifted his chin. "We remain behind schedule. It is more imperative than ever that we recover the lost sevendays. It will be difficult. Of our three DOP-Cs, one is assigned to the geology team surveying the crevasse. That will leave the rest of the planet exploratory teams with two DOP-Cs until the flyers complete planetary grid mapping. Bright Star and the Thirteen Systems cannot wait. We cannot mine vistrite without settlers to provide support to the miners. We cannot land settlers without reliable surveys and maps."

***

Bran reclined in the corner of the sofa, one arm curled around Adriana. Beyond his cabin window the planet was half in shadow, the dark blue smear of the mountain range disappearing into blackness. Pulling her stockinged feet onto the cushions, she settled against his chest. At the other end of the sofa, Blue was slowly blending with the green-and-blue pattern of the throw she had claimed.

Resting his chin on her curls, Bran sought a means to broach his intent. "How long do you think it will take to finish the ground surveys of the plains?"

"No more than a sevenday. With what we sampled from the crash, another two days on the ground should complete the catalog to the extent needed for settler decisions." She threaded her fingers with his. "I plan to petition the first officer for militia support to set monitors in the forest. It is huge, and, for the moment, not desirable for settlement. Visual records should suffice until we have more opportunity."

"I think you can rest assured your petition will be granted." He took a breath. "As named members of the vistrite discovery team, our added honor bonus is astronomical. Combined, we can purchase Blue's pack territory and whatever buffer zone you consider wise with the proximity to vistrite."

He felt her stiffen. In the Thirteen Systems, comingling assets was far more intimate than physical congress. It was not a consort alliance, or wedlock, but it was a commitment to a future beyond the next sunrise.

Her fingers squeezed his. "Yes. And, once I have a better understanding of the area, it might serve as a nature retreat. A quiet place when commerce has taken too much from us."

His heart lifted at that *us*, even with it spoken so tentatively. He wanted to push but, he had waited this long, he could tread softly a bit longer. "Raleigh expects that instead of allowing the *Nightingale* to return to Fortuna for resupply, Monsignor Lucius and the other Bright Star governors will accelerate the timetable for allowing supply transports to the Thirteenth system. It may be a half year before we return to the beaconed expanse."

"I am not surprised. Finding vistrite changes everything. They will need a stellar transport platform for the excavation equipment. Even a small one will take at least a month to assemble once the components arrive."

"It does not trouble you to remain in the Thirteenth System?"

She half turned, a soft smile curving her lips. "I am more than content where I am." She looked past him to the dark planet. "It turns out that the Thirteenth System holds far more wonders than I imagined." She lifted bright eyes. "And by that, I mean you."

Cupping her chin, he gave voice to his heart's desire. "You are far more than I ever hoped to find on this journey. As for wonders, none will exceed finding you, but I am eager to explore what else this system holds. With you."

Her eyes glowing, she placed her hand over his. "Yes."

About EG

I write from the world around me, and the world around me is full of color.

Award-winning author EG Manetti has always enjoyed a vivid imagination and occasional scribbling.

Her epic science fiction series, **The Twelve Systems Chronicles**, blends the intrigue and danger of space opera with the passion and social rigidity of historical romance. The ten-volume series has received four **Paranormal Guild Reviewers Choice Award**s, and seven *InD'tale* **RONE** (Reward for Novel Excellence) nominations, with five volumes awarded finalist badges. *Shield Bearer: Thornraven, Volume 2* received the **2021 RONE** for Science Fiction.

Elemental Fire: The Hidden Realms #1, her first venture into fantasy, combines her favorite aspects of urban fantasy, paranormal romance, and action/adventure genres. It received a 2023 RONE Silver Medal for Fantasy/Urban Fantasy.

She is currently working on a Twelve Systems Chronicles spin-off series, Thornscore, where popular secondary characters receive their happily-ever-after. She is also planning a sequel to *Elemental Fire* for release in 2026.

A former information technology project manager, EG resides in Florida with her beloved (often confounded) husband and their somewhat neurotic Jack Russell Terrier. She writes as often as possible, cooks exceptionally, and gardens adequately.

Made in United States
Orlando, FL
08 June 2025